MURDER AT THE LIGHTHOUSE

AN EXHAM-ON-SEA MYSTERY

FRANCES EVESHAM

Boldwood

First published in Great Britain in 2020 by Boldwood Books Ltd.

Cover Design by Nick Castle Design

The characters and events described in the Exham on Sea Mysteries are all entirely fictitious. Some landmarks may strike fellow residents of Somerset, and particularly of Burnham on Sea, as familiar, although liberties have been taken with a few locations.

A CIP catalogue record for this book is available from the British Library.

Paperback ISBN 978-1-80048-013-1

Large Print ISBN 978-1-80048-014-8

Ebook ISBN 978-1-80048-011-7

Kindle ISBN 978-1-80048-012-4

Boldwood Books Ltd
23 Bowerdean Street
London SW6 3TN
www.boldwoodbooks.com

1

UNDER THE LIGHTHOUSE

The autumn high tide discarded Susie Bennett under the lighthouse, on the beach she'd avoided for twenty years.

A fierce autumn wind whipped across Exham beach, driving sand rain in Libby Forest's face. It tore at her hood as she trudged across the expanse of deserted beach. The locals knew better than to brave this morning's weather. Libby shivered. Newly arrived in Exham on Sea, she'd underestimated the strength of the storm. She tugged her hood closer, as the wind snapped strands of wet brown hair across her face.

No wonder Marina, one of the handful of people who'd welcomed her to the town, had jumped at her offer to walk Shipley, the Springer Spaniel. Excited by the storm, Shipley pulled at the lead, dragging Libby towards the lighthouse.

She'd never seen a building like it. White-painted, perched on the sand on nine wooden legs, the lighthouse looked hardly strong enough to withstand a breeze, never mind this gale.

The dog ran around Libby, wrapping the lead round her legs. She stepped out of the tangle and hesitated. The dog pulled harder and her arms ached. Marina had forgotten to mention the animal's lack of training.

Could Libby let him run off some of his energy? She didn't want to lose Marina's pet. It seemed hard enough to be accepted in a town like this, where everyone seemed to know other people's business, and Marina was chairman of music club and the history society. Her opinion counted in Exham.

'I'll chance it,' she told the dog. 'You're pulling my arms out of their sockets.'

Free from his lead, the animal raced in excited circles, twirling and spinning, ears alternately flat against his head or standing at right angles, like aeroplane wings.

As Libby squinted into the wind, Shipley skidded to a halt, right by the lighthouse. She ran to catch up, and he barked, whiskers quivering, head pointing.

'What's that?' Libby gasped as she reached his side. 'Looks like an old sack. Still, we'd better take a closer look.' The tide had receded, almost out of sight, leaving a layer of mud surrounding the lighthouse. It stuck to Libby's boots, dragging her down, sucking at her feet as she picked her way to the shapeless bundle, testing every step.

'It's a person. A drunk, I suppose,' Libby said. 'We'd better wake him. He'll freeze, in this weather.'

The drunk lay awkwardly, half supported by one of the lighthouse legs.

Libby braced herself for a mouthful of abuse from the drunk, and shook one of the leather-jacketed arms.

The drunk slid noiselessly to the sand. The spaniel nosed it, whining. 'Quiet, Shipley.' Libby squatted beside the body, brushed sopping wet hair from an icy cheek, and searched the neck for a pulse. 'It's not a man, it's a woman.'

Shipley howled into the gale. Rain beat down on Libby,

sliding into her hood and slipping down her neck, but she hardly noticed. Her stomach felt hollow.

She staggered up, legs trembling. 'It's a woman, and she's dead.'

She scanned the beach, but they were alone. Libby shivered. 'We'd better tell the police.' She tugged a mobile phone from an inside pocket and fumbled, jabbing 999, calling the emergency services.

'Hello, do you need fire, police or ambulance?'

This was only the second corpse Libby had seen, and an image of the first floated into her head. She'd seen her dead husband, Trevor, laid out at the hospital. The memory triggered a painful mix of horror and guilty relief that he was dead and she was free at last.

She wiped her hand across her wet face. This was no time to think about Trevor. She looked closely at the body. Who could it be? A local? No one Libby recognised, but then, she hardly knew anyone here apart from Marina, a few members of the history society and Frank Brown, the owner of Brown the Bread, the bakery where she worked part-time.

Slim and tiny, about Libby's age, the dead woman wore skin-tight jeans. A brown ankle boot encased one foot, but the other was bare, the expensive footwear long gone. The woman's lips were fuller than nature intended. Cosmetic work in the recent past? Drenched hair half concealed a small, neat face with a turned up nose. A line of darker hair, along a parting on the side of the head, suggested highlights; a proper salon job, not a do-it-yourself.

Libby peered into the puddles under the lighthouse, looking for a handbag, hoping for clues, but the sea had left nothing behind.

I shouldn't touch the body again. Libby knew the rules: everyone did. *Don't disturb the scene*. She should wait for the police to arrive, but something about the woman's arm, tucked at such an awkward angle into a jacket pocket, nagged at Libby. It wouldn't do any harm just to give it another small nudge, surely?

She twitched the sleeve and the arm jerked. Libby, startled, jumped back and almost tripped over Shipley. 'Just rigor mortis,' she muttered. She pulled again, harder. The stiff hand popped out of the pocket, rigid, fingers pointing to the bleak, wide Somerset sky. A chunk of plastic tumbled from the jacket.

Libby whispered, 'Sorry,' as though the dead woman could still hear. Shipley nudged the woman's face, and Libby pulled him back, clipping the lead to his collar.

The sudden, shocking wail of police sirens brought an officer, younger than her own son, running down the beach. Libby held out one hand, as if to protect the body. 'Be careful.'

The young plainclothes officer raised an eyebrow above intense blue eyes and waved an ID card under Libby's nose. 'Detective Sergeant Ramshore. Step over there and leave it to us now, please, madam. We need to clear the scene. The constable, here, will ask you a few questions.'

A female, uniformed police officer led Libby and Shipley along the beach, up a short flight of steps to a seat on the promenade, its roof providing some shelter from the wind and rain. As she answered the officer's gentle questions, Libby gazed through relentless rain, past the tiny pier with its deserted kiosk, to the brightly coloured houses and shops of the town.

The dead stranger still lay, forlorn, on the beach, a small plastic ring with a pink stone tumbled beside her on the sand.

2

COFFEE AND CAKE

'There's no reason to cancel the meeting.' Marina folded her arms, enclosed in the purple sleeves of a wafty silk caftan, across an ample chest. She settled comfortably in her chair and beamed at Libby. 'Folk will arrive in a moment.'

The local history society meeting was due to begin. Libby had dashed home from the beach to Hope Cottage, her new home. She shut Shipley in the hall while she located Fuzzy, her marmalade cat, safe in the airing cupboard, and changed, grabbing the first skirt and jumper she found.

Retrieving the cake she'd baked yesterday, juggling the tin as Shipley pulled on the lead, she hurried past the empty children's play park to return the dog to his owner and deliver refreshments, as promised, for the meeting.

'I'm sorry we took so long,' she'd gasped as Marina opened the door.

'Did you?' The other woman had raised an unconcerned eyebrow. She hadn't been worried about her pet, then.

Marina had taken the lead, winced as Shipley shook water all over her hall carpet, and shooed the dog into a room at the back of the house, closing the door firmly. Libby hoped his bowl was full – Shipley deserved a good feed.

She wished, now, she'd taken more trouble with her appearance. In her hurry, she hadn't bothered to dry her hair properly and it hung in a tangle of brown round her face. She tugged at the hem of her sweater as she told Marina about the dead woman on the beach.

Marina shrugged. 'I expect the woman was on drugs. There's no need for you to worry. The police said they'd keep you informed, so they'll let you know.'

'Yes, but...' Libby wasn't confident Detective Sergeant Ramshore would bother.

'Now, listen to me.' Marina was not the newly retired deputy head of the local primary school for nothing. She understood command. 'You need a distraction, Libby. Come into the kitchen. We'll slice up your cake and forget about this down-and-out.'

'She didn't look like a down-an-out,' Libby mused, waving a knife. 'Her jacket was leather – expensive, I think, but not new.' She remembered the dark roots to the woman's hair but kept that to herself. She felt oddly protective towards the unknown woman.

She was grateful to Marina. The woman had been kind, taking Libby under her wing, and persuading her to join the society. Somehow, and Libby was unsure how Marina had achieved it, she'd talked the newcomer into providing cake for the history society meetings.

'Everyone's sure to love it, dear. People are already talking about your cakes. Frank Brown has never had so many customers, and we're all looking forward to seeing your book.'

'Hmm. If I ever finish it.'

Marina had waved away such nonsense. Writing a book about celebration cakes, full of photographs, must be the easiest way possible to make a living. 'Anyway, you can practice your cakes on us.'

As a result, Libby supplied at least one elaborate confection for each meeting. She had to stand on her own feet now her husband was dead and she needed all the publicity she could get.

Marina sampled a slice of today's contribution, a pineapple and coconut upside-down cake with a cream cheese frosting. 'Delicious. Your best yet.' The doorbell rang. 'There you are.' She beamed. 'It's too late to cancel now. Angela's here.'

Soon, Marina's grand drawing room was full.

'Quite a turn out,' Angela Miles murmured in Libby's ear. 'Almost everyone's braved the rain today. They've heard about your adventure. News travels fast in Exham.'

Libby had only met Angela once before, at a previous society meeting, but she instinctively liked her. While Marina overpowered with her confidence and easy assumption that she knew best, Angela was calm, with a dry sense of humour.

'Good heavens,' she said now. 'Samantha Watson's gracing us with her presence.'

Libby had not met Samantha, but Marina had described her. 'Our resident intellectual. She's a solicitor, and she tells me she can complete the Telegraph crossword in half an hour.' Marina had snorted. 'She also claims to answer most of the questions from University Challenge. If you believe that, you'll believe anything.'

Samantha sashayed into the room. As Marina introduced her to Libby, she let her eyes roam over Libby's unkempt hair and everyday clothes.

'Pleased to meet you,' she murmured, lowered herself into a chair and crossed one long leg over the other. Her sheer tights hissed as she smoothed a tight pencil skirt over shapely knees.

'We don't often see her at these meetings,' Angela murmured. 'Her time's too valuable.'

Libby bit back a laugh as Angela continued, 'She doesn't come to many social occasions with the likes of us.'

'One of my clients cancelled an appointment, so I've just popped in for a minute.' Samantha explained, raising a hand, as though granting the society a favour. 'Such a shame, by the way, another tragedy on the beach.' She glanced at Libby. 'I hear you found the body.'

Marina said. 'A visitor stuck in the mud, I suppose, when the tide came in. How foolish. When will they learn not to go walking over the riverbed?'

Angela explained to Libby, 'You can only see it when the tide goes out. The coast guard often rescue people. They put red flags on the beach, but strangers don't take enough notice. It looks calm, but the sand turns treacherous and it can suck you in.'

Libby shuddered.

'Ships have been caught out, as well. The town's had three lighthouses over the years, to keep them from running aground.'

'Three?'

'The low lighthouse where you found the body, the Round Tower on the esplanade – that's not in use any more, and neither is the High Lighthouse near the sand dunes.'

'Good grief. I thought I was coming to such a safe, quiet little town.'

Angela smiled. 'I don't think any coast is truly safe, do you? When the gales blow in the autumn, you can't ignore the force of nature. I lost a summerhouse last year.'

Marina joined in, 'And my fence blew down. Luckily, I was insured.'

Samantha allowed Marina to place a slice of cake on her plate. She cut it neatly into tiny squares and popped them, one after another, into a lipsticked mouth, a little pink tongue flicking out to chase stray crumbs.

'Quite nice,' she pronounced.

Marina's pent up excitement overflowed. 'Such a shock, finding a body. It gave me palpitations just hearing about it. You must be in *pieces*, Libby dear.' Her voice sunk to a dramatic whisper. 'Imagine, a dead body, lying there all night, out on the beach, in such dreadful weather.'

Samantha cleared her throat to focus attention back on herself. She had a glint in her eyes. 'I spoke to Detective Chief Inspector Arnold on the telephone a while ago.'

Angela murmured, 'So that's why she's come.' She leaned closer. 'Samantha hears all DCI Arnold's secrets.' She whispered, 'Pillow talk.'

'You mean, they're an item?' Libby murmured. 'I'm sure Marina told me she was married to that builder, Ned.'

Angela nodded. 'She was – but I think she finds a senior police officer more to her taste these days. She's something of a social climber – that's why she married Ned in the first place. His family used to own Mangotsfield Hall, the Victorian stately home. One of Ned's ancestors was the earl, but the title died out years ago and the family sold up. You don't often see Ned and Samantha together, nowadays.'

'I rang him the other day. I'm hoping he'll sort out my bathroom in Hope Cottage,' Libby said.

'Hope Cottage,' Marina had overhead. 'Such a dear little place, tucked away in that funny little lane.'

Samantha coughed, raising her voice above the chatter, an edge to her voice. 'Detective Chief Inspector Arnold told me the woman is Susie Bennett.'

A shocked silence followed. A glow lit Samantha's face. She had her audience's full attention now.

Marina's jaw hung open. 'Susie Bennett?'

Samantha beamed; smug mouth curved in a complacent smile. 'That's right, Susie Bennett, the folk singer – or rock singer, was it?' She shrugged elegant, cashmere clad shoulders. 'The Susie Bennett who used to go to school with some of us.' She let her eyes rest on Libby, who was never at school with 'us'. 'The Detective Chief Inspector thinks she committed suicide.'

Seriously? He's already decided? In three hours? Libby pressed her lips together and kept her thoughts to herself.

Everyone in the room seemed to have known the dead woman. Marina gasped. 'Oh good gracious me. Susie Bennett! She hasn't been back for years. Whatever was she doing here?'

Angela set down her cup of tea. 'Libby, Susie is Exham on Sea's most famous export. She went to America and sold millions of records, back in the eighties. She was in a band called Angel's Kiss. I remember, because my name's Angela. Actually, Angel's Kiss was a cocktail, I believe.'

Marina interrupted. 'I remember one of their albums. It came with a drinking straw attached to the cover. That lovely song, 'What's In a Name,' was one of the tracks. Susie played the guitar and sang, and there was Guy with a violin and another boy – what was his name, now? Oh yes, James. He was on keyboards.'

Samantha fiddled with her pearl necklace. 'I don't want to be unkind, but Susie, or Suzanne, as she was in those days, was rather — how can I put it — strange. You know, she had a big voice, big blue eyes, and a great deal of blonde hair, but there was no brain there at all.' She waved, dismissing Susie as a failure. 'She left school with absolutely no qualifications.'

'We were all madly jealous of her, to be honest,' Angela admitted. 'Off we went to University or started work as trainees at Barclays Bank or Marks and Spencer, while she made records. She married a fabulously wealthy record producer, but the marriage didn't last long. I don't know about the rest of you, but I haven't seen or heard of her for years.' She sighed. 'We were rather unkind to her, I'm afraid.'

When the teapot was drained and the cake plate empty, the meeting broke up. 'Next time,' Marina said, 'we really must talk about history.'

Finally, only George Edwards, the sole male member of the society, remained. He wrapped the last slice of cake in a paper napkin to take home and, breaking his silence, begged Libby to write down the recipe for his wife, who was at home nursing a cold and laryngitis. 'She'll be sorry she missed everything.'

Libby collected the empty cake tin and left. Angela walked by her side, heading for her car. 'I wonder what Suzie was doing in Exham, after all these years.'

3

ROBERT'S DISCOVERY

Recessed spotlights picked out the details of Libby's beautifully equipped kitchen as she made coffee, using the state-of-the-art, instant hot water dispenser, installed last week. She pulled out mixing bowls, sieves and scales, and settled down to a trial run of the perfect, elaborate, light-as-air cake she was developing. If it turned out as beautifully as she expected, it would make a wonderful cover picture for the follow up to her recent book, 'Baking at the Beach.'

It was this room that had persuaded Libby to buy Hope Cottage. Facing south, always either sunny or cosy, perfect for a baking fanatic. Without a qualm, she'd sold her husband's treasured trainset, lavishing every last penny it fetched on her workplace.

Their son, Robert, had been horrified. 'You can't sell that, Mum. It was Dad's pride and joy.' It had filled a room in the London townhouse.

'I know, but I'm moving to Somerset, to a cottage. There won't be room for everything – me, my professional kitchen, and a trainset. I have to earn my own living now your father's gone.'

Robert had sighed. 'He didn't leave you that badly off, did he? You never said...'

Libby smiled. Robert was such a worrier, and he'd adored his father – she could never tell him the whole truth about the man. She'd never told anyone how Trevor had treated her, criticising her clothes, telling her she was fat, constantly making excuses to prevent her friends coming to the house. It had taken all her strength to keep his bullying from Robert and Ali.

She sometimes thought Ali, her daughter, suspected the truth. Ali had been keen to leave home for Bristol University, six months before Trevor died, and she'd not returned home during those months, although she'd telephoned Libby every week.

Now, at least, the money from Trevor's railway had been put to good use. From the KitchenAid mixer on the granite counter, to the gleaming rows of heavy bottomed pans that hung on the wall near the range cooker, Libby adored every inch of the room.

She'd once confided to Trevor the dream of setting up her own chocolate shop. Trevor had taken off his glasses and glared, his nose less than an inch away from her face.

'Don't be so stupid.' Libby had flinched as saliva hit her face.

'Throwing good money after bad. Besides, I expect to find you at home when I come back after a hard day.' He sneered, replaced the spectacles right on the end of his nose, poured a tumbler of whisky and settled down to read the newspaper's business section. Libby's new kitchen would have been enough to make him choke on his drink.

What a pity the bathroom didn't reach the standard of her kitchen. The orange made her feel sick every time she saw them. In a day or two, Ned, the builder, was coming to get rid of the horrid, 1970s bathroom.

The phone rang as she shaved fractions of an inch from the sponge cake. Robert was excited. 'Mum, I've got news.' Libby's heart leapt. He was getting engaged at last. There would be a wedding. She'd need a new dress, and a hat...

'Are you listening? I've discovered a new great, great, great aunt, and what's more, she lived in Somerset.' Libby sighed and cast a despairing glance at the meringue mixture she'd whipped to exactly the right consistency, as it collapsed, ruined.

When he was a studious, serious teenager, Robert preferred history to football and Latin to art. Libby had little interest in the Forest relations, Trevor's ancestors, but Robert worshipped his father. He never saw Trevor's dark side.

Now, Libby tried to be interested. 'Do tell me about it, darling.'

'You know Dad always said his family were landowners?'

'Mm-hm.' Did he? Libby swallowed a mouthful from a second cup of coffee. She added a slug of whisky to settle her nerves and licked her lips.

'Well, I've found someone called Matilda Forest, who was a maid at a stately home.' Libby almost wished Trevor were here now. An ancestor in service – how he'd hate that. So much for landowners.

Robert was still talking. 'And the house is in Somerset, near you. A place called Mangotsfield Hall. It's open to the public. Maybe we can all visit? Sarah's keen and we can come down in a couple of weeks.'

Sarah was Robert's girlfriend, and her parents lived in the West Country. That had helped, when Libby insisted on selling the family home and moving to Somerset. 'At least, Sarah and I can come and see you and her parents at the same time,' Robert had admitted.

Her interest sparked by the mention of Mangotsfield Hall, Libby asked. 'What did you find out about this Matilda?'

'Well, she had to leave the Hall because she was pregnant –

the family wouldn't have her in the house. She didn't go far, just to Wraxall. The baby kept her surname, but, get this, Mum, his Christian names were Stephen Arthur, and those were the names of the earl who lived in the house.'

Libby chuckled. 'Are you telling me your father's ancestor was what they used to call, 'No better than she should be,' after hanky-panky with his lordship?'

'Honestly, Mum, Dad would be mortified.' Even Robert laughed at the thought.

'So, he would,' she agreed.

Libby said, 'By the way, I had an adventure, yesterday.'

'You did?'

'No need to sound so surprised. I'm not that old, yet.'

'Sorry.'

'But I found a body on the beach.'

He sounded puzzled. 'What sort of a body?'

Libby took a breath, enjoying the moment. 'A dead one.'

'What?' His reaction was everything Libby had hoped for.

By the time Robert rang off, keen to pass on such interesting gossip to Sarah when she came home from work, he'd squeezed every detail from his mother.

The phone rang again. Still smiling, Libby picked it up. 'Hello, darling, what did you forget?'

The deep voice on the other end of the phone brought her back to reality with a thud. 'Is that Mrs Forest? It's Detective Sergeant Joe Ramshore here.'

Libby let the silence draw on for a moment. She really didn't want to talk about the body under the lighthouse again. She was exhausted from answering Robert's questions. She let out her breath in a long sigh. 'Yes, it's me.'

'Well, I'm ringing to thank you for your help today.' Joe Ramshore was the young detective from the beach. The one with blue eyes and a superior expression. 'We wanted to let you know we've identified the lady you found.'

'Susie Bennett?'

'Oh. You've heard, then.' He sounded put out. 'We think we know what happened, Mrs Forest. I thought you'd like to know that the deceased—' He coughed. 'I mean, Susie Bennett, seems to have been alone when she died. I didn't want you to worry. It was all an unfortunate accident, or at the worse, intentional.'

'Intentional?' Samantha had said it was suicide. Libby shivered. Setting out to drown yourself in the autumn gales was a strange way to take your own life. Why not swallow a few pills, or jump off Clifton Suspension Bridge?

The detective was still talking. 'Well, I'm afraid she had an awful lot to drink. We think she-er-vomited and choked. The forensic examiner found traces. We couldn't see them on her clothes – the rain had washed them away. No one else involved. It must have happened the night before you found her, though it's hard to tell the time of death, what with the cold water, and so on.'

'Oh.' What an anti-climax: to die like that, so foolishly. 'What about the ring?'

'The ring?' He sounded puzzled. 'Oh, yes, that bit of plastic on the sand. It was just a toy ring, nothing valuable. I expect it was in one of her pockets.'

'But—' Libby broke off. No need to confess to moving the body. She compromised. 'I just wondered why she'd have a plastic ring in her pocket.'

'Oh, I see. Well, we don't know.' The police officer's tone was measured, pedantic. 'She wouldn't have been wearing it, would she? It's a child's ring.'

Libby rolled her eyes. She could work that out without his help. 'Yes, but—'

'We had a look at it, but there wasn't anything we could use: no fingerprints or anything, I mean. The weather saw to that.'

Libby insisted. 'I meant, did Susie Bennett have a family?'

'Ah, I see what you're thinking. You're wondering if she has young children.'

Libby, exasperated, crossed her eyes and waggled her head. Good thing the police officer couldn't see her. 'Yes.'

'I can put your mind at rest on that, Mrs Forest. We don't know of any family. Of course, we're getting records over from the US, because her husband was American.'

'Yes, yes I heard that. You know, from people in the town.'

'Well, it's a small place. I'll let you know when the inquest comes up. The coroner will want to ask you some questions. Nothing you need worry about. It's not like going to a criminal court.'

'No, well, thank you. Oh,' Libby exclaimed.

'Yes?'

'I wondered how she got there. Did you find a car, or anything?'

The police officer sighed. 'No, but there are buses, Mrs Forest. Exham's not that remote, you know. She was a local lady, probably came back to the place she grew up, if she wanted to end her life. That's not unusual, you know.'

His voice was warmer now. 'Try to put it out of your mind, Mrs Forest. I know it's upsetting, but these things do happen, I'm afraid.'

Libby put the phone down. Too restless to go back to the spoiled meringue, she climbed the stairs to the bathroom. A hot bath might relax her.

She tried to unwind by reading a magazine, but her mind drifted away to the image of Susie Bennett, drenched and cold, slipping sideways under the lighthouse, in dreadful slow motion.

The scene played over and over in her head, like a YouTube video on a never ending loop.

It didn't ring true. Surely, no one would choose such a place, on a stormy night, to drink alone.

It was no good. She stepped out of the bath. How could she leave it at that? The police might be satisfied there was no foul play, but Libby wasn't. If they weren't going to try to discover the truth, she would find out for herself. Was Susie's death really an accident, a deliberate suicide, or something much worse?

4

FUZZY'S DISGRACE

The early morning sun peeped, pink and coy, over the horizon, as though the past two days of storms and wind belonged to another era. Libby walked Shipley along the beach in the opposite direction from the lighthouse. She wasn't ready to repeat yesterday's disastrous trip.

She'd tossed and turned all night, unable to forget Susie's face, the pink plastic ring, or the nagging suspicion that Susie might be a victim. She hoped the walk would clear her mind.

A dozen fishermen, with all the time in the world, leaned against the sea wall, rods extended into an ebbing tide. They nodded, mumbling a greeting as Libby passed and George Edwards wrapped a fish in newspaper, holding it out to Libby. 'For breakfast.'

She took the package, stowing it safely in her backpack, hoping it wouldn't leave too pungent a smell.

'How's your wife?' She asked, wondering if she'd ever meet the woman.

'On the mend. The voice is back, more's the pity. By the way,' he called Libby back. 'She loved the cake. Let me have a copy of

your book, will you? Do for her Christmas present.' *Poor Mrs
Edwards, was that going to be her only gift?*

When Libby arrived home, Fuzzy left the airing cupboard to
follow her mistress into the kitchen, meowing pitifully.

'Are you hungry, then?' Libby picked her up, nuzzling the soft
fur. Fuzzy allowed this display of affection for a count of three,
then squirmed, squeaked and wriggled away. For some reason,
she'd never taken to Libby, always preferring Trevor. Trying to
please, Libby opened a can of salmon.

Full, content and purring, Fuzzy left the house via the cat flap
in the back door. She'd work off breakfast chasing the mice, frogs
and birds that had made the neglected garden their home long
before Libby moved in.

'A wildlife garden,' Libby explained, when Ali phoned. 'No
need to weed the borders.' Her daughter, like Robert, had been
nonplussed by Libby's crazy move from London to a quiet seaside
town.

Libby downed a second mug of tea, shrugged on a bright red
trench coat guaranteed to brighten her mood, and climbed into
her tiny, eleven year old Citroen, to drive to work at the bakery.

Reversing out of the drive could be a challenge. The road she
lived on wasn't exactly busy, for most traffic used the parallel
main road, but it was ever-changing. Mums and Dads walked
their children around the corner of the road each day, heading
for the nearby primary school. Teenagers, ears plugged with
headphones, materialised suddenly from behind parked vans,
mouths open in amazement at finding cars on the road.

It was too early for young people, today. They'd still be struggling
awake. Libby switched on the ignition and reversed the car, hands
light on the wheel, head turned to peer through the rear window.

A flurry of barking exploded nearby, like breakfast time at the boarding kennels. Libby jumped, foot jerking on the accelerator. The vehicle lurched. She jammed on the brake, but it was too late. The rear of the car crumpled with a sickening crunch as it hit the lamp post opposite her house.

Libby threw the door open, to find her exit blocked by a dog. It reached almost to her shoulder as it struggled on its lead, howling like a wolf. 'Be quiet, Bear.' The grey haired man on the other end of the lead yanked the dog back to let Libby out of the car. 'Sit down.'

The dog subsided, panting, saliva dribbling from its tongue. Libby slammed the door. 'That animal should be locked up.'

The man bent over the rear of the Citroen. 'I'm afraid there's a dent.'

'Of course there is. Your dog's a menace.'

He straightened up, towering several inches above Libby. 'He's not mine,' he said. 'I hope you're not hurt?'

Libby pointed. 'Just look what you've done to my car.'

'Forgive me, but you were driving. All Bear did was bark at that cat.'

Libby followed the pointing finger. Her shoulders slumped. Fuzzy crouched on top of the fence, fur fluffed out, laser beam eyes trained on Bear. The dog, tantalised by a tormentor so close, yet out of range, howled again.

If a cat could be said to smirk, that's what Fuzzy did. Libby groaned. 'Oh. That's my cat,' she blurted. 'Well, my husband's. Late husband.' The back of her neck was hot. She tried to smile. 'I'm afraid Fuzzy's nothing but trouble.'

'Fuzzy?' The man grinned.

'Her fur goes fuzzy in the rain.'

'Well, I'm afraid there's not much we can do about the car. Your insurance will cover it.' The stranger smiled, waved and went on his way. Bear barked once more, in a forlorn attempt to entice Fuzzy down from the fence.

Libby rubbed at the dent. The paint was intact, and it was only a tiny bump. A garage would knock it out in minutes. She straightened up. That man could have apologised a bit more, though. Who was he? Where had he come from? She hadn't seen him before but he looked familiar, nevertheless.

She glared at Fuzzy. 'Last salmon you'll get from me.'

5

THE BAKERY

Frank Brown brought a tray of bread, steaming and fragrant, through from the kitchen at the back into the shop just as Libby arrived. 'Morning,' he grunted. 'What's the latest on Susie Bennett, then?' He scooped up a pile of baking trays, already on the way back to the kitchen. 'They say her last album will be back in the charts, now she's dead. Too late for her, but it makes you wonder who'll get all those royalties.'

Libby had never heard him talk so much. His communication was usually limited to 'yes', 'no', and, 'those loaves need to come out of the oven', but under the gruff exterior he had a kind heart. Marina had told her Frank was a staunch supporter of the Rotary club and its charitable work.

The shop's work experience teenager leaned on the counter, twirling a stud on her lip. Libby secretly called her Mandy the Goth. 'My Dad went to school with her.'

Libby laughed. 'So did half the town, I gather.'

'I heard you found her. Was it gruesome? Was there much blood?' The girl's eyes, black with layers of kohl and mascara,

were enormous in the white-painted face. Two silver rings deco-
rated one nostril above purple lips.

'Mandy.' Frank put his head round the door. 'Get on with
those sandwiches before the rush starts. Wash your hands and
put some gloves on.'

Mandy sighed, rolled her eyes, hitched up a long, black lace
skirt and went back to scraping egg mayonnaise into baguettes.

'Dad said she was always asking for it,' she muttered under
her breath, glancing towards the kitchens. 'Sexy but stupid, he
said.'

The bakery did a roaring trade. Almost everyone in town
dropped in, keen to look at the person who found the body. Frank
beamed. 'That's the most sandwiches we've sold since Jeremy
Clarkson came down to drive off the pier.'

By eleven o'clock, Libby's feet ached. Her head throbbed from
the effort of repeating, 'I just happened to find her', and, 'The
police say there's nothing suspicious'. When the queue no longer
snaked out of the door and around the corner, but had shrunk to
one or two stragglers, she retreated to the kitchen. Mandy could
serve the final few High Street estate agents.

Frank removed his white hat, still unusually talkative. 'Can
you finish that new ginger and lemon recipe by this afternoon,
Libby? I reckon it'll be a winner.'

'Mmm. Just need to tweak the frosting. A bit over-sweet, I
thought.'

'You're the expert. It'll sell like hot cakes.' Libby grimaced.
Frank made the same joke at least once a week. 'Funny thing,' he
went on. 'Millions of people watch cooking programmes on TV,
and half of 'em don't know how to turn on their ovens. Still,
mustn't grumble. Where would the business be if everyone did
their own baking, eh?'

Frank left to drive the van, loaded with filled rolls, to a nearby conference centre. Libby took a deep breath, drinking in the smell of freshly baked bread. She tied on a clean apron, and set about testing the new recipe, relishing the familiar, satisfying tasks of measuring sugar, beating eggs and sifting flour. She'd persuade Frank to let her put the new confection in her next book.

Mandy joined her. The teenager's earlier good humour seemed to have evaporated. Libby opened her mouth to tell her to stay in the shop, ready for new customers, but the look on the girl's face changed her mind. Mandy's lip trembled. Libby said, 'We'll hear the bell if anyone comes.'

Mandy grunted, tipped a bowl of risen dough onto a bench top and pummelled it as Libby watched. Nothing relieved angry feelings better than making bread. It had been a favourite therapy during her miserable marriage. What had upset the girl?

'Everything all right?' Libby asked.

Mandy said nothing. Libby let it go. She recalled her own children as teenagers, not so long ago, grunting and taking offence at everything she said. At least that phase had passed.

For ten minutes, only Mandy's effortful gasps and the whirr of the food processor disturbed the peace of the kitchen. The corners of Mandy's mouth still drooped. She sniffed. Libby had an idea. 'Why don't you make the frosting?'

As Mandy dumped the bread dough back into a stainless steel bowl for its final proving, she explained.

'I've weighed everything out, but the sugar needs watching.' The teenager scraped dough from sticky fingers, shrugged and picked up a wooden spoon. 'Make sure it all melts before you turn up the heat. That stops the mixture turning into a gritty mess.'

Mandy, eyes on the saucepan, stirred. 'Mrs Forest?' She sounded hesitant.

'Mm-hmm.' Best not to sound too interested, and perhaps the girl would share whatever was worrying her.

'Dad threw a knife at Mum.'

'A knife?' Libby stiffened, sugar spilling from the spoon.

'It was only a knife from the table – not a carving knife or anything.'

Libby gulped. No wonder the girl was upset. 'Is your Mum OK?'

Mandy nodded. 'Think so. She says it's not the first time, nor the last. He missed, anyway.'

Libby lowered the spoon and took Mandy by the shoulders. 'She needs to tell the police.'

The girl shrugged Libby's hands away and swiped a sleeve across her eyes, smudging black mascara across one cheek. 'She won't. I've told her. She says he doesn't mean it. He's sorry, later.'

'Mandy, that's rubbish.' Libby closed her eyes, fighting memories. She took a long, slow breath. 'Of course he's sorry afterwards. They always are, but it happens again.' Fingernails bit into the palm of her hand. 'Has he ever hit you?'

Mandy tossed her head. 'He tells Mum it's her fault for making him angry, but anything sets him off. It was just about watching football on the telly, yesterday.'

Libby pulled out a chair and eased on to it. She'd had just such a stupid row with Trevor. They'd argued – shouted – about nothing, and she'd thrown his dinner in the bin. He'd cracked the TV remote control against her shoulder, all his strength behind the blow. His face, contorted with fury, sometimes appeared in Libby's dreams. She'd been terrified he'd hurt the children.

'Mandy.' She took a moment to control her voice. 'Mandy, if your mother won't do anything about it, then you should leave the house. You're old enough.'

Mandy bent over the saucepan. 'I think the sugar's ready to boil.'

Libby handed over the sugar thermometer. 'Think about it. I've got spare beds at my house if you need them.'

Mandy sniffed and rubbed her nose but said no more. Libby let it go. The girl had to make up her own mind.

The doorbell tinkled. Libby left Mandy at the hob, watching sugar boil in the pan, and stepped into the shop, pulling on a pair of clean white gloves. 'Can I help you?'

Tall, grey haired, a little older than Libby, and dressed in a long blue overcoat, the new arrival smiled. 'Good morning.'

Libby stared. 'It's you. The man with the dangerous dog.'

'So it is. We seem to have got off to a bad start.'

'I should say so.'

He grinned. 'I gave Bear a good talking to before I handed him back to Mrs Thomson.'

Libby's lips twitched. 'Quite right. He needs to learn to behave. Fuzzy's a bit of a menace, of course.'

'Well, to be honest, I liked the look of Fuzzy. I admire a cat that stands up for itself. Bear doesn't agree.'

Libby looked at the blue eyes. Yes, definitely familiar. Where else had she seen them? 'Did you want a sandwich? Or cake?'

'Just a ham salad baguette, please.' He patted his middle. 'Have to watch the weight, these days.'

Mandy arrived from the kitchen. She'd redone her mascara. 'The frosting's ready, Libby.' She stopped. 'Hello, Mr Ramshore.'

Libby looked from one to the other. 'Ramshore. Like the detective sergeant?'

He smiled. 'My son.'

6

COFFEE AND SUSPICION

This new Ramshore's first name turned out to be Max. 'My parents were Norwegian.' That explained the blue eyes.

'I thought I owed you a cup of coffee. I wasn't too gracious, earlier. Bear is much too big and loud, and I should have managed him better, though your cat caused the trouble.'

'He didn't—'

'Anyway,' he broke in, 'let's not argue again. There's a coffee shop further down the road. Can I buy you a coffee?'

'I don't know. Mandy would be alone in the shop.'

'I can manage, Mrs F. We're quiet, now.'

'Well, if you're sure.' There was something very pleasing about Max Ramshore's eyes, and his smile took years off his face. Libby wondered how old he was. Fifty? No younger than she was, anyway. 'Just ten minutes.'

Libby chose a table in a corner the coffee shop and shrugged off her coat while he bought two lattes.

'What breed is Bear?'

'Carpathian Sheepdog. Very gentle, like many big dogs, but he needs an incredible amount of exercise. He belongs to my neighbour, Mrs Thomson, really. Her husband kept him on the farm, but old Eric had to go into a care home before he died – dementia, I'm afraid. I own the farm now, though I don't work it myself. I look after Bear when he gets too much for Mrs Thomson, which is quite often. She still lives in the old farmhouse, down the lane from me.'

'Well, anyway.' Libby wasn't ready to forgive him, or Bear, completely. Besides, she was suspicious. 'Did you know I worked in the bakery? I'm sure you didn't just happen to walk in today.'

'No, to be honest, my son told me about you.'

'The detective sergeant himself? What did he say?' She glared. 'Aren't the police supposed to keep things confidential?'

'He just suggested I look out for you, on my marathon Bear walk this morning. He thought you might be upset, after that business on the beach. Then, you had your little accident.'

'Caused by Bear.'

'And Fuzzy.' His eyes twinkled. 'I can see we're not going to agree on that. Anyway, I felt bad, so I asked one of your neighbours where you might be going. It's a small town, you know.'

'You can say that again.' Where did looking out for each other stop and nosiness begin? 'Have you always lived here?'

He nodded. 'I went to school with Susie Bennett, you know.'

Libby laughed.

'What's funny?'

'Everyone I've met here went to school with Susie, but she doesn't seem to have many friends.'

'It's a small town. We all grew up together. Susie wasn't in my year, she's a couple of years younger, but I knew her.' Libby waited for the inevitable slur on Susie's character, but he surprised her. 'She was a nice girl. A difficult family, though.'

'Oh?' Libby hesitated. 'You're the first person I've heard say anything good about her.'

'Who have you asked? Wait. Let me guess. The Townswomen's Guild?'

'No.' Libby's face burned. 'The local history society, actually. They all knew her at school.'

'And didn't approve.'

'Maybe they were jealous?' She was thinking aloud.

He stirred coffee with a long spoon. 'Susie was too pretty for her own good, and too ready to believe everything the boys told her. You know how teenage boys can be. They try it on with girls, then if one says yes, they pull her reputation to pieces. That's how it was with Susie. Hardly any friends, just boys who wanted her for one thing. She had a terrific singing voice, though.'

'I hear her album's likely to make a fortune.'

He crumbled a coconut macaroon onto the table. 'I bet the music company are thrilled. They don't care how they make a profit, do they?'

'She went to America, before she became famous, didn't she?'

'It all started here, though. Small local gigs at first. It was Glastonbury where they got their big break.'

Libby shivered. 'Glastonbury. I went once. Cold, wet and smelly, as I remember.'

He laughed. 'Not everyone's cup of tea. Still, it's great place for up-and-coming bands. Mickey Garston, the big American music producer, heard Susie there, signed up the band and married her. It all happened fast. He whisked her away and the next we knew; she was on the cover of million selling albums and on TV.'

'What about her family?'

'All dead or gone away. No Bennetts left in the town.'

'That's sad.'

'Typical story of a small-time girl with a turbulent life, I'm afraid. The marriage with Mickey Garston didn't last long. They split up years ago, but she never married again.'

'No, she wasn't wearing a wedding ring when I found her.' Did Max know about the plastic ring? Had Joe told him she'd moved the body?

Max Ramshore drank the last drops of coffee and set the cup down with care. 'My son mentioned a different ring. He said you seemed bothered by it.'

'Bothered? No, why should I be?' Her face was burning.

'Come on. What are you hiding? I'm not the police, you know.'

'No, but your son is.' She bit her lip. Now it sounded as though she'd committed a huge crime. 'OK. I moved the body. I pulled her hand out of her pocket and the ring fell on the beach. That's all. I know I shouldn't have touched her, but she looked so – well – vulnerable, I suppose. I wanted to help. Does that sound crazy?'

'I told you, I'm not the police.' It was his turn to hesitate. 'Truth is, I know a bit more about Susie than the others around here. It's private information, and maybe I shouldn't tell anyone, but it makes me think there was something more going on than her committing suicide.'

Libby licked dry lips. 'D'you mean, you think she was murdered?'

'Mmm. Sounds a bit melodramatic, doesn't it?'

Libby thought about it. 'That scene at the beach – it wasn't like a suicide.'

'The police have it down as an open and shut case, at least unless the coroner disagrees at the inquest.' He shook his head. 'Frankly, if no one does anything, she'll be a statistic: just another girl who grew too rich and famous and couldn't handle it. I don't want to let that happen.'

'What is it you know?'

The man blinked and looked away. 'Not here. We need to talk

somewhere more private. Can I take you to dinner tonight? There's a restaurant near Taunton where they know me. They'll let us have a quiet table.'

Libby bit her lip. 'All right.' She stood up. 'I've got to get back to the shop. Pick me up at seven?'

7

DINNER

Libby changed her dress three times before seven o'clock. It was stupid to feel so nervous. *I'm behaving like a teenager.* She hadn't been out alone with a man since Trevor died. The last thing she wanted was an entanglement. Not now, as she started to build the life she'd always wanted.

The linen shift dress was elegant, and a shade of pale rose that brought colour to her cheeks, but it wouldn't keep her warm, it creased too much, and the neckline was too low. She tossed it on the bed. This wasn't a date, after all. The man had only asked her to dinner to discuss Susie. Maybe she was an old girlfriend.

Libby tried a silk dress with a high waist and flared skirt that made her look girly. 'Mutton dressed as lamb.' she told Fuzzy, who rolled on the linen dress, covering it with ginger and white hairs.

Libby shooed the cat away and pulled out a pair of black evening trousers, matching them with a white shirt. There, that didn't give out any awkward signals. It was neat and business-like, but the trousers were well cut and the subtle embroidery, like damask, made them chic enough for evening. A silver chain round her neck, a heavy silver cuff on her wrist, and a squirt of scent completed her preparation, just in time. The bell rang as she left the room.

He was early. Libby ran downstairs, stomach fluttering, took a breath and opened the door. Mandy, hair wildly back combed into an unruly bird's nest, rested a foot on the doorstep as if poised for retreat. In one hand, she hefted an unwieldy backpack with a black t-shirt spilling out of the top. The other hand was at her mouth, teeth tearing at a black-painted fingernail. She dropped the hand long enough to whisper, 'Did you mean it? Can I really come to stay?'

'Of course you can stay.' Mandy staggered into the hallway and Libby took the bag. 'I don't think it's safe for you to go home, if you're frightened of your father.' She took the bag. 'Good heavens, whatever have you got in there?'

Mandy made a sound halfway between a laugh and a sniff. 'My laptop. And some books.'

Books? Mandy? That was a surprise. 'Well, you're welcome to stay. I could use a lodger, here. There's a spare room. Does your Mum know you're here?'

'I didn't tell her.' Mandy's fingernail was back in her mouth. She looked like a frightened child.

'You should let her know. Won't she worry?'

'I'll ring her later. Dad won't be back tonight. He's going out drinking with his old mates and staying over at the Watson's place.' Maybe Samantha would keep an eye on Mandy's father: help him stay out of trouble. Libby would ask Max Ramshore about Mandy's dad this evening. He'd know what to do. His son was a police officer.

Mandy, gaining confidence once the front door closed, perched on a stool in the kitchen, gazing around the room, eyes wide. 'Wow. What a place, Mrs Forest.'

'Call me Libby. Now, I must go out this evening, but the bed's made up in the spare room. I won't be late. Make yourself at home and help yourself to anything you can find.'

Mandy was scooping walnut brownies from a tin when Max Ramshore arrived. 'Don't worry about me.' She looked from one to the other, the hint of a smile on her face. She'd be on Facebook before they were out of the drive. By tomorrow, everyone in town would know they'd been out for dinner.

Libby's companion drove a comfortable, well-used Range Rover. Bear lay in the back, greeting Libby with a bark. 'Hello to you, too,' she said, tugging his ears.

Max Ramshore raised his eyebrows. 'Hope you don't mind if Bear comes too. He likes the White House.'

The restaurant was by the river, a string of tables lining the bank. There was an autumn chill in the air, but the wind had dropped. Still, it was a good job she'd brought a warm jacket. Libby rejected the polite invitation to eat inside. She liked the dark of the evening, and lights illuminated the scene. Bear made himself at home, disappearing into the reeds on the riverbank, searching for a succession of sticks for Max to throw.

'If you grew up in Exham, Mr Ramshore, you must know just about everybody in town.' Libby had spent all her life, until now, in West London. 'I meet a new person one day, like Mandy at the bakery, and the next day I drop into the newsagent and find her mother works there. It's like a spider's web.'

'I wish you'd call me Max,' he said. 'You're right. We're a small community. If you need a job done, you can always find a friend or relative of someone you know, who can help.'

'I'm asking Ned Watson to renovate my bathroom. What do you think?'

He tapped his fingers on the table. 'He's probably the best option. There's always Bert, Mandy's dad, if you want it done for cash with no questions asked. But I wouldn't advise that. A bit crooked, is Bert. Ned Watson's better. He undertakes building and plumbing. Tell him you know me, and he'll give you a decent price.'

'Tell me more about Mandy's father. Bert, you said?'

Max grimaced. 'The man's a bully. He was like it at school. No one's lunch money was safe.'

Libby peeked at Max's shoulders, broad as a boxer's. Her lips twitched. 'I bet yours was.'

He smiled. 'I can look after myself. Since school, Bert's been on the dole most of the time, though he makes plenty by cleaning windows: cash payments only, of course.'

'Is Mandy's mother safe? Won't he hurt her?'

Max took a sip of Beck's Blue non-alcoholic beer. 'I'm not sure. Bert goes down the pub with a bunch of his loser pals, gets drunk and takes it out on Elaine. The police are called round there from time to time.' He shrugged. 'Usual story. Wife takes him back every time. Refuses to press charges. She's had a black eye or two.'

Max's own eyes glinted, cold as ice. 'I try to keep an eye out for Elaine. Bert listens to me, so long as he's sober. We go back a long way, but I'm not always successful. One day, he'll go too far.'

Libby swallowed. 'Well, she'll be OK tonight. He's staying with the Watsons.'

Max laughed. 'Samantha would never have let Bert stay if she was at home. She ruled Ned with a rod of iron until they split up.'

'Anyway, Mandy's safe with me. Her father won't even know she's there.'

'He'll hear soon enough: you can't keep secrets in Exham on Sea, you know.' Max topped up her glass. 'Don't worry about Mandy. She's eighteen, old enough to make her own decisions.'

He swished beer around his glass. 'What about you? How did you get here?'

'My husband died.'

'I'm sorry.'

She met his eye. 'Don't be. I'm not.' His eyebrows shot up and Libby laughed. 'Sounds dreadful, I know, but he was my big mistake. My parents warned me.' She hadn't listened, and she'd never told them they were right. 'He turned out to be one of those controlling husbands. Another bully, like Mandy's father. That's why I was keen to get her away from their house. I know what it's like.'

'I'm so sorry.' Max's eyes were dark with sympathy, and Libby's stomach gave a little lurch.

'I know it sounds awful, but when Trevor had a heart attack, I cheered inside. At last, I could work, have my own life, make friends and live where I chose. I chose Exham on Sea.'

She raised her glass. 'To my new life.'

'Now,' she put the menu to one side. 'We didn't come here to talk about me. What can you tell me about Susie Bennett?'

8

Max drummed his fingers on the table. 'The thing is, Susie kept in touch with me after she left. I used to live and work in Bath, in one of the banks, and Susie came in one day, before she left for America, and opened an account.'

'Was she rich?'

'Not rich then, though she was later, but I don't think she ever trusted Mickey. I tried to stop her going away with him.' Max's eyes were focused on his plate. Did he still hold some sort of a candle for Susie? It would explain why he was the only person in Exham on Sea with a good word to say for her.

'She wouldn't listen. Said she could handle herself but wanted to be sure there were funds somewhere safe, that only she knew about, in case she, or anyone else, ever needed them.'

Their steak arrived and Max stopped talking, refilling Libby's glass with wine and taking a deep draught of beer. Libby sliced into her food, watching blood trickle from the rare steak.

'Or anyone else,' she murmured. 'What could she have meant by that?'

Max shrugged. 'She wouldn't say. Just told me it was her

secret and she'd let me know when she wanted the money. That's all there is to it.'

'That's all?'

'I shouldn't even be telling you.' The sharp edge was back in his voice.

Libby ignored it. 'I'm glad you did. What happens to the money now?'

'There's been a pretty big pot waiting for Susie, but she never used it. She never came back, just contacted me from time to time to check on the interest. In the early years, we spoke about every six months. She talked about needing it soon, but after a while, she stopped contacting me.'

'When was that?'

'Oh, six or seven years after she married. It was about the time of her last album. You remember, *Twilight over the Sea?*'

Libby did remember. Susie's dark contralto voice blending with a plaintive guitar in sad songs of love and loss. Her best work, the critics said. 'She never made another album, did she?'

'No, that was it. She lived the rock and roll lifestyle with Mickey: plenty of drugs and booze. They broke up a few years later and she wrote to me again, asking me to keep the account open. She said she'd probably not need it, anyway. That was the last time we were in contact, apart from the statements sent by the bank. I haven't seen her for years.'

Libby took a chance. 'You were pretty close to Susie, then, if she trusted you with her money?'

His eyes narrowed. 'What gossip have you been listening to?'

Libby held his gaze, keeping her voice steady. 'I don't listen to gossip, but you're the only one I've met so far who knew Susie after she left.'

Max picked up a dessert spoon from beside his plate, twirling it in his fingers. His eyes slid away, looking out over the hills. Libby pulled her jacket more tightly round her shoulders.

'Susie and I had a business relationship. It was no more than that.'

'But you'd have liked it to be more?'

Max's eyes narrowed. Libby flinched at the steely undertone to his voice. 'It's none of your business, Mrs Forest.'

She gripped her hands under the table. She took a gamble and murmured, 'Did your wife know how you felt about Susie?' A man as attractive as this must be married. Libby discovered she wanted to know.

Max's eyes were stony. 'We're divorced.'

'Because of Susie?'

He gave a sharp laugh and drained his glass with a flourish. 'Oh, Mrs Forest, how very inquisitive you are. Do you think I murdered Susie Bennett?'

'I don't know, but I'm sure someone killed her. I'm just trying to find out more about the people who knew her. You're one of them. I thought you wanted to help.'

'Of course I do. You'll have to make up your own mind about me, but for what it's worth, I didn't kill Susie, even though I was no model husband. To answer your question, Susie was just one of the reasons my wife and I quarrelled. But there were plenty of others. Now, if you've had enough to eat, we'd better move inside. The wind's getting up and I'm freezing cold.'

Sure enough, a gust of wind blew napkins from the table and raindrops splattered the cloth. Max rose to his feet, calling Bear back from the river. The dog arrived, wet, muddy and smelly. Libby shivered. 'Maybe we'd better just leave?'

9

WALNUT BROWNIES

Max drew up behind the Citroen. 'You'd better get that dent fixed. Try Jenkins' Garage, it's the best around this area.'

'I suppose you were at school with Mr Jenkins.'

'As it happens, I was.'

'Another member of The Band of Brothers?' Libby climbed out.

'I suppose you could call it that. We look out for each other.'

'Well. Thank you for dinner. And, good night.'

The house lay quiet, the kitchen clean and tidy. Mandy was on her best behaviour. How long would it last? Libby, unsettled, fell into bed, her stomach full of good food and wine, and slept heavily until morning.

The phone startled her awake. 'I've been thinking about that money of Susie's.' Max didn't bother to ask how she was. This relationship was strictly business. Libby swallowed a stab of disappointment, yawned and focused on his voice. 'Anything she saved will be part of her estate and go to her heirs. I'm wondering who they might be.'

The smell of burnt toast and the sound of scraping rose from the kitchen, and Libby's mouth watered. She tried to concentrate as Max talked. 'I'm going over to the States. I've got Susie's old address. I think we need to let people know what's happened.'

'Isn't that a police job?'

'No, not if there's no foul play in the case, apparently, and no grieving husband or children. Someone needs to find a solicitor, or attorney, or whatever they're called in the US, and sort out wills and so on.'

'So, you're going to do it?'

'Er – yes. Well, there's no one else, is there? It'll take ages if we wait until after the inquest and anyway...'

He let the words hang in the air but Libby knew what he was thinking. Justice for Susie. 'I'm off to Heathrow now. There's a flight this afternoon.'

'Already? What about Bear? Who's going to walk him?' *Shut up, Libby, what are you saying?*

'I've left him with Mrs Thomson. He'll have to wait for his exercise until I get back.'

Libby let the silence grow. It wasn't her job to look after that huge dog. She groaned. 'I'll go and rescue him. I don't see why he has to suffer.'

'Libby, you're a treasure.'

'I know I am. You'd better let me know anything you find out. And Max, there's one question we have to answer.'

'What's that?'

'If she's been living in the US since the 1990s, with no contact with anyone in England, what the heck was she doing on Tuesday on the beach at Exham on Sea?'

She put the phone down. *And why are you so keen to go to the States? What are you up to?*

She rang Ned Watson, mentioned Max's name and asked him for a final quote for the bathroom. He was business-like. 'I like a week to do a bathroom. You don't want to rush it.' He'd come around tomorrow to get started. Libby, used to long waiting lists for any work in London, was impressed. She couldn't wait to see the back of the orange tiles and avocado green bath.

* * *

Mrs Thomson's old, tumbledown house lay just outside town, surrounded on three sides by green fields, cattle and a green knoll that rose in a rounded hump from the Somerset levels. A flock of sheep and three or four horses speckled the slopes.

Libby peered up the lane. A few stray leaves, hardy enough to withstand the recent gales, still clung to the branches of a row of trees – horse chestnuts, perhaps. The tracery of branches framed a neat, white-painted building. That must be Max's place. Libby whistled. Max Ramshore lived in style. *Mr Lord of the Manor.*

What was it he did, exactly, that he could leave at such short notice to go to the States? He'd left the bank, but he was way off retirement age. Or, was he going to America for some other reason, using Susie as an excuse?

Beyond Mrs Thomson's' house, dunes led down towards the golf club and beach. The nine legged lighthouse must be nearby. Libby dragged on the brake, eased out of the car, tugged the battered boot until it opened with a screech, and rescued a box of walnut brownies. Tucking it under one arm, she scanned the net curtains for signs of occupancy.

She thumbed the doorbell and waited. No answer. She rapped on the wood of the door and leaned harder on the bell. No one in. Maybe she'd do some snooping round Max's house, as he was away.

As she stepped back, Bear bounded around the corner, greeting her with the enthusiasm of a long lost friend. With a super-human effort, she kept her feet, pushing the dog's wet nose away from her face. The door creaked open.

An aged head appeared in the gap between door and frame, hearing aid peeking from behind each ear. Libby recognised the old lady's Victory Roll hairstyle, popular at the end of the Second World War. Her great aunt used to wear one. 'Mrs Thomson?' Libby raised her voice. Deafness must be a blessing to anyone who lived with this sheepdog and his ear-splitting bark, but it was going to make conversation difficult.

The lady of the house screwed up her eyes. 'Are you the dog walker for Bear?'

So far, so good. 'Max Ramshore sent me. He said you'd like me to come and help with Bear while he's away. I've brought some brownies.'

The door closed. A chain rattled and Mrs Thomson pushed the door wide, beckoning with one hand as she untied her apron with the other. 'Come in, come in. I'll make a cup of coffee and see if we've got any biscuits. You must be hungry, coming all this way.' She led Libby through the house, talking all the time.

All this way? From Exham?

'I've brought brownies,' she repeated.

'Yes, we get a lot of townies here. They like to walk on the Knoll.'

10

ANNIE ROSE

Mrs Thomson's long, low sitting room looked out over the dunes. The windows were small and wooden, long overdue an update to double glazing. Libby shivered. The wind from the sea must blow straight through the crumbling wood. She could smell the salt from here.

Mrs Thomson shook her head at Libby's bawled offer of help in the kitchen, pointed to the sofa and went out. Libby tried to remove dog hairs from the tapestry cushions decorating the sofa, changed her mind about sitting down, and stepped over to the window. It took an effort of will to make herself look to the right, along the beach to the lighthouse.

The view encompassed the whole beach, from the pier to the lighthouse and beyond. The tide was out again, leaving the building's stumpy legs exposed in the mud. Libby released her breath in a relieved sigh. There was no body in sight, today.

Mrs Thomson returned, balancing a tray painted with cats. China cups and jugs rattled as she lowered it to one of the side tables. Vases, silver framed photos and dog-shaped ornaments teetered on the piano. Pictures of Bear standing alongside a bent, aging man hung on the walls. Mr Thomson?

His widow poured coffee and brought a cup to Libby at the window. 'We've got three lighthouses in Exham, you know.'

'Three?' Libby sipped the hot coffee.' It seemed the three lighthouses were a source of pride to local people.

'Yes.' Mrs Thomson stretched knobbly, arthritic fingers. 'There's one on the beach, up there,' she nodded to the right. 'That's where they found Suzanne, the other day.' Libby set her cup and saucer down on the table nearest to the hairy sofa and sat. She could brush her jeans later.

Mrs Thomson took a brownie. 'These are nice, dear. Did you make them yourself?'

Libby smiled. 'You've heard about Susie Bennett, then, Mrs Thomson?'

Her companion shook her head, her brow folded into a criss-cross of lines. She looked about to burst into tears. 'Oh, yes. Such a shame, a lovely girl like Suzanne.'

Libby bit her lip. Mrs Thomson was old and widowed. Maybe asking questions, getting her to relive the past, would be cruel.

Before she could decide, Mrs Thomson was talking. 'I knew her before she was famous, when she was a little girl, singing at the Christmas parties the vicar used to put on over there.'

She pointed through the window to a small, squat church that lay almost on the dunes. 'Suzanne, we called her. I don't hold with shortening names that were given at a proper Christian baptism. The young people do it all the time, these days. You never know who's who. My name's Marjorie, and I never let anyone call me anything different, not even my Eric.'

'Did you know Suzanne well?' Libby steered the conversation back to the past.

'My Eric used to play the piano while Suzanne sang. Such a

pretty little thing, she was, all curls and a big smile.' There were tears in the old lady's eyes.

What had she thought when Susie grew up and developed a taste for boys and fast living? 'Did other children go to the parties, too?'

'All the boys and girls were there. There'd be dancing and games, Suzanne would sing, and Maxwell would play the saxophone. You know Maxwell, don't you? Calls himself Max, nowadays. Of course you know him. What am I thinking? It's Maxwell sent you round to walk Bear.' She leaned on the arm of the chair, pushing down for support and staggering to her feet. 'I'm getting forgetful, that's my trouble. Where did I put Bear's lead, now?'

Libby cut in. 'Please tell me more about Suzanne.'

Mrs Thomson narrowed her eyes. 'Why do you want to know about her? From the press, are you?' She pursed thin lips. 'I know the girls from the local paper. You're not one of them. Are you from the Western Daily Press?' Her voice rose. 'Nosey people, those reporters. That Jeremy Abbott from Weston super Mare barges his way in without so much as a by-your-leave. He came yesterday evening, but I didn't open the door to him. Never do, after six o'clock, not at my age. I like to settle down in front of my telly.'

She gave Libby a hard look, as though trying to remember who she was. 'Anyway, I've nothing to say to you, so you'd better be getting off.'

PHOTOGRAPHS

Judging by the unhealthy, deep red in Mrs Thomson's face, the elderly lady could be on the verge of a stroke. Libby held out her hands. 'No, no. I'm not a reporter. It's just that – well, I found Susie's body, Mrs Thomson. Suzanne's, I mean. I was walking my friend's dog on the beach.'

'Hm.' Mrs Thomson stopped in mid-gesture. She stared hard at Libby, suspicious. Satisfied, she sank back into the chair, the livid colour slowly ebbing from her face. 'I suppose Maxwell wouldn't have sent you round here if you were with the papers. He has his faults, that one, but at least his heart's in the right place.'

Libby hesitated. She didn't want to risk hurting the old lady, but she needed to know more about Susie. 'You must have been proud of Suzanne?'

'Mr Thomson used to keep all the cuttings from the newspapers when she went to the States. Who'd have thought little Suzanne would make such a big name for herself?'

Libby took a shot in the dark. 'Did she keep in touch after she left Exham?'

'Oh yes, she used to send me all her records. Albums, they call them nowadays, of course.'

'Or downloads.'

'Pardon?'

Libby wished she'd kept her mouth shut. 'Nothing.'

Mrs Thomson was talking again, 'She sent a card at Christmas, as well, every year, regular as clockwork. All except for that one year.'

'Which one was that?'

'The year the little girl died. It must have been, let me see, the little girl was seven, so that was back in the early nineties. She wrote and told me about it, but no cards that year. Not surprising. Poor Suzanne, it broke her heart.'

Coffee scalded Libby's throat. 'Little girl? She had a daughter? That explained the pink ring. Libby had been sure there must be a child.

'Oh yes, she had a daughter in America. With Mickey what's-his-name. Big record executive, he was, or some such. Annie: that was the little girl's name. Annie Rose. Pretty little thing, she was, just like her mother. Here, wait, I've got a photo, somewhere.'

She pattered from the room; old green slippers soundless on the patterned carpet. Drawers opened and closed in a different part of the house. Mrs Thomson returned, clutching a red photo album and Libby shifted along on the sofa, making room. Heads together, they flipped through pages of photos: babies, houses, older children.

'Here we are.' Mrs Thomson pointed at four photos protected by a filmy, plastic sheet.

A neat, handwritten date and caption accompanied every image. 'My Eric put all our photos in an album, labelled and everything. He was like that. Always neat and tidy.' Mrs Thomson peered round the room, maybe half hoping to see the late Mr

Thomson in his usual chair. 'The farm was the best in the county. Our Herefords won prizes.' Her shoulders slumped. She sighed, misty eyed. 'All sold, now.'

Afraid the old lady was slipping into reminiscing about the farm, Libby tapped a finger on the photo at the top left of the page. 'Is this Suzanne?'

'That's her. Still at school, then.' Libby caught her breath, shocked to see a young Susie smiling in the photo, very much alive. Under the lighthouse, she'd been wet, bedraggled and dead. Nevertheless, this was the same person, no question. There was no mistaking the neat nose and arched eyebrows.

Mrs Thomson moved on to the other pictures. 'Here she is, on stage in America.' Two tall youths, one bowing a violin, the other behind a keyboard, each young face taut with concentration, dwarfed the singer. Despite her tiny stature, Susie's personality sprang from the photograph. She glowed, alive with the joy of performance, an enormous guitar slung round her long, white neck.

'This one's her wedding photo.' Mrs Thomson's voice jerked Libby back to the present. 'And this—' one gnarled finger touched the last photograph, light as a caress, 'is little Annie Rose.'

Libby let her eyes slide down to the image of Susie's little girl. The child was a miniature of her mother. Hair so fair it was almost white, she struck a dancer's pose, toes pointed, arms in the air, delicate in a tiny version of her mother's fringed skirt and full-sleeved blouse.

Libby dragged her gaze from the dead child's enchanting dimples and looked at the wedding photo. So, that was Mickey, the husband. He loomed over Susie, heavy arm pulling her off balance, crumpling the puffed satin wedding dress. The bride gazed up at her new husband adoringly, while he smirked at the camera, stealing the moment like a spoilt child.

Still, being self-centred and arrogant didn't mean he was responsible for Susie's lonely death. If Mickey was in Los Angeles on the day she died, he couldn't have killed her. Libby hoped Max would take a good look at the man's alibi. 'Mrs Thomson, do you know how Annie Rose died?'

'Oh, dear. I'm afraid the poor thing drowned.'

Libby's head spun. Perhaps Mrs Thomson was confused. 'No, I mean Annie Rose, not Suzanne.'

'That's right. She fell in the swimming pool.' Mrs Thomson's eyes were very bright. 'They all have swimming pools, out in California. It's so hot, you see. It broke Suzanne's heart.' Her smile trembled. 'We never had children, Eric and me. Suzanne was like the daughter we never had. We'd been so happy for her, with her little girl, doing so well, and then, Annie Rose died. It was quite dreadful. Eric never got over it.'

Libby's stomach lurched. Had she jumped to conclusions? Maybe Susie had drowned herself, after all, still heartbroken, choosing to end her life as Annie Rose had lost hers. Perhaps the police were right.

She struggled for words. 'How did you find out?'

'They rang, from America. Mickey's secretary, I think it was, said Suzanne was too upset to talk but she wanted us to know.' Mrs Thomson took out a tiny white handkerchief and wiped her eyes. 'There, it still upsets me, dear. I'm sorry to make a fuss. You see, it all happened so far away. And now this...'

She blew her nose again, pocketing the scrap of cotton, standing, shrugging her shoulders. 'Well, these things happen. I'll make more coffee.'

Mrs Thomson clattered in the kitchen. Libby flipped backwards through the pages of the album. She found a photo of a Christmas tree, piles of presents and rows of kids. They were about eleven or twelve years old, Libby guessed. The vicar beamed in the centre of the back row. She looked closer. There was Susie – Suzanne – in the front row, a brace running along her teeth.

The tall, gangly boy standing beside Susie looked familiar. Yes. It was Max. Mrs Thomson returned, tray in hand, and leaned over Libby.

'Look, there they all are. Most are still here, or hereabouts. There's Maxwell, of course, and Benedict who's married to Samantha. The one with the broken tooth is Alan – Alan Jenkins. Oh, look, there's Angela...'

She broke off as the doorbell rang. Libby jumped to her feet, glad of an excuse to avoid more coffee. Her insides were awash. 'Don't worry, Mrs Thomson. I'll open the door.'

An elderly woman on the doorstep wrinkled her forehead, perplexed to find an unexpected stranger in her friend's house. 'Oh. Is Marjorie in?' A cake shaped parcel, wrapped in tin foil, peeped from her basket. Libby ushered the newcomer in, made her excuses to Mrs Thomson, grabbed Bear's lead and left them to their memories.

12

BEAR WALK

Libby gripped Bear's collar when they arrived home, hauling him back as she unlocked the door. The last thing she needed was a confrontation with the cat. She shouted for Fuzzy, but as usual there was no response. That animal came only when she chose, and she could be anywhere. Probably out for the day, finding dogs to torment. Libby wasn't about to leave Bear outside, digging up the tiny garden. She wanted the huge animal where she could see him.

She shut the door to the sitting room. He wasn't going in there either, no matter how much he whined or scratched the door. Libby's heart sank. The animal barely fitted into Hope Cottage, and she couldn't let him into the kitchen. Not if she wanted a hygiene certificate so she could sell her own food.

He'd have to stay in the hall. She looped the lead over a door handle to keep him from the stairs.

'Sorry, Bear. It's only for a while.'

He deserved a reward. Food? She scratched her head. She'd never owned a dog. What with Shipley's wild chasing on the beach, and Bear's size and quantity of drool, she was learning, fast.

Did the aging, forgetful Mrs Thomson remember to give him regular meals? That might be why Max had taken the dog under his wing. She should offer him something to cheer him up, and there was steak in the fridge – a treat for the weekend. Libby had planned to share it with Mandy, her new lodger, but the tiny rent she was asking for wouldn't cover it, anyway.

Libby dropped the rump steak in an old bowl and Bear leaped on it with enthusiasm. 'You're either hungry, or greedy.' She set a bowl of water near the food.

The builder, Samantha's husband, arrived on time, built like a wrestler, with enormous thighs and shoulders, his biceps tight inside a sleeveless t-shirt. He squeezed past Bear. Comfortably full, the dog was taking a nap, stretched out along the hall, snoring happily. Ned considered the bathroom, sucking his teeth and accepting Libby's offer of cake. 'These avocado suites were put in during the seventies,' he said. 'Don't see them around very often, these days.' He laughed.

She sighed, 'I can't wait to get rid of the tiles.'

'It'll take me a week,' he announced, once he'd measured the room. 'I'll email the quote for the work, while you choose the units. Here.' He thrust a shiny catalogue in Libby's hands, swallowed her last brownie in one bite, and left.

Head teeming with plans for a spa bathroom that she knew she could not afford, Libby climbed the stairs to the study, opened her laptop and pulled up a list of a hundred and twenty emails. Most were junk. A long page from her daughter tempted her, but she moved on. Ali would ring if there was a problem. This was a news bulletin. She'd enjoy it later.

Ah, there it was. Max had checked in, as promised. She'd exchanged emails with him before he left for the States and been secretly hoping to hear from him. She'd liked the man's eyes, and she was touched that he'd chosen to look after Mrs Thomson and Bear.

She felt like she had as a teenager when a boy she fancied smiled at her. *This is ridiculous. I'm far too old for that nonsense, and a respectable widow of two years. Max and I are collaborating for the sake of Susie.*

She forced herself to concentrate on the email.

Staying in luxury in Hollywood

he gloated.

Contacted Mickey's company and got an appointment to see him this afternoon. Told them I was an old friend of Susie's and it was personal and urgent. Will let you know what happens.

Libby snorted. Luxury in Hollywood would mean five-star glamour. Flowers in the room, champagne on ice. Libby's family holidays had been camping in Scotland or a week in a chilly holiday cottage or, when the kids were teenagers, caravan holidays in France. Trevor never wasted money. Max, it seemed, had plenty.

She knew he had retired early, and she suspected he'd been more senior than a 'bank manager', judging by the sizeable farm he'd bought from the Thomsons. He had contacts in America – maybe he was a kind of consultant, charging thousands for a day's work.

Libby closed the laptop, retrieved Bear from the hall, wiped up the water he'd splashed on the wooden floor and set off, anorak hood firmly in place against the weather. It had turned nasty again. The wind and rain grew stronger every moment. It was going to be a rough afternoon and probably a stormy night. Summer seemed a very long time ago.

She rejected a walk on the beach, heading for the countryside, and choosing a couple of fields with no livestock. She wasn't taking any chances, although Carpathian Sheepdogs, she'd discovered online, were peaceful, placid animals with an affinity for sheep, able to roam long distances in the Romanian hills to keep their charges safe.

She found a stick and threw it. Bear charged away, fur flying, grasped it in his teeth with hardly a pause, raced back and dropped it triumphantly at her feet. Libby laughed aloud, pulled his ears and threw the stick again. Fuzzy would never dream of such undignified behaviour.

'Oi. You.' The voice came from behind. 'What the devil d'you think you're doing?'

A short, squat man wearing a waxed jacket and flat cap appeared at Libby's side. 'We're not doing any harm.' How dare he shout at her? This was a public footpath.

Oh. No. Now Libby thought about it, she realised it wasn't. She'd left the path some way behind. Still, there weren't any crops here to be trampled, and no sheep or cows. She'd brazen it out. The man's face was very red, his nose enormous and lumpy. *Drinks too much.*

'That dog's not on a lead. I could shoot him.' The man's eyes were small. He narrowed them into angry slits.

'You haven't got a gun.'

'Didn't say I was gonna shoot, did I? But I could.'

They summed each other up. Libby stood as tall as her five foot four inches allowed and glared, hiding triumph as the man's gaze dropped. 'What you doin' with Bear?'

'You know him, then?'

''Course I know him.' He called out, 'Hey, Bear.'

The dog raced over to lick his hand, happy to transfer his allegiance from Libby.

'Oh. Well, I'm walking him for Mrs Thomson. Max asked me to.'

'Ah. Max.' He drew the word out. The grin was insulting. 'Friend of yours, is he?'

'Not really. I like walking dogs. I'm just helping out Mrs Thomson while Max is away.'

The man nodded; the smile even broader. 'Gone far, has he?'

About to tell him to mind his own business, Libby stopped. Instead, she tried her best smile, head on one side, eyelashes fluttering. 'I don't know him well. He seems very busy. I've no idea what he does all the time.'

The man laughed. 'Max has his fingers poking into all sorts of pies. You be careful, now, a nice lady like you.' His eyes travelled up and down Libby's body.

Glad of the shapeless anorak, Libby tried another tack. 'Do you live around here?'

'Over yonder, t'other side of the hill. Want to come and see?'

'Why not?' Was she mad? Libby straightened her shoulders. She could look after herself.

They trudged along the lane without speaking. He was definitely the strong, silent type. They turned the corner, but saw was no sign of a house. The edge of the village began a hundred yards down the road, and the nearest building bore a garish sign, 'Jenkins Garage.' Libby's spirits rose, despite the missing apostrophe. That was the garage Max had mentioned. 'Is that yours?'

'Yep. Alan Jenkins at your service, Ma'am.' There was grime under his nails and oil stains on his coat. He was not a farmer, after all. He'd been stringing her along. Libby wouldn't make much of a Sherlock Holmes. She hadn't even recognised him as one of the boys in Mrs Thomson's photo album.

He might be a useful source of information. He knew Max, Susie and the others. In any case, her car needed him. 'Maybe you can help me. There's a dent in the back of my car.'

'Jag, is it?'

'I wish. Citroen.'

'You bring it round; I'll see what I can do.'

Libby took Bear back to the house. She found Fuzzy in the airing cupboard where she'd been hidden in a nest of Libby's towels all the time the builder had been there. She shut the dog in the hall, barricading the stairs with kitchen chairs, and took the car round to Alan Jenkins at the garage.

He pursed his mouth. Ramping up the bad news so he could overcharge her, Libby decided.

'Tell you what,' he said.

'Yes?' She braced herself.

'Seeing as you're a friend of Max's, I'll do it for nothing.'

'What? Don't be ridiculous. Why would you do that?'

He grimaced. 'The thing is, Mrs-er...'

'Mrs Forest.'

'Mrs Forest. The thing is, I owe Max a favour, just at the minute. I reckon, seeing as you and he are good friends, like, this 'ere'll pay it off.'

Libby's blush rose hotly up her neck. 'We're not good friends. I told you, I hardly know him.'

''You were out at the White House t'other night, and that's a fact.'

'Yes, but...' More evidence of the speed of the town grapevine. Libby's words tailed into silence as her brain raced. 'Well, maybe we are friends. Max has plenty of friends.'

'Yes, and I wouldn't want to be on the wrong side of most of 'em.'

Libby swallowed. 'So, what's the favour you owe him?'

'Now, that would be saying.'

The man was putting on a good local yokel act, Libby had to hand it to him. 'Come on, Mr-er-Alan. If you want me to help you get on the right side of Max, you'd better tell me a bit more, or else I'll give you a cheque and tell him you threatened me.'

'I never did.'

'I know that, but Max doesn't.' Libby coughed, fighting a snort of laughter. Alan Jenkins had turned pale.

'All right.' He looked around, to check they were alone. 'There's been some ringing.'

Libby tried to look intelligent. 'Ringing? With – er – um...'

'Broken-down cars fit only for scrap, sold for next to nothing, tarted up, clock turned back, sold on to nice unsuspecting ladies, like you.'

Together, they eyed Libby's car. 'It came from a proper Citroen garage, I'll have you know. A long time ago.'

He wiped his hands on the front of his overall. 'Anyway, the garage got in a bit of trouble with a Bristol gang and Max – well, he sorted it out for me.' Max had enough clout to scare off a gang of criminals, had he? Alan Jenkins picked up an oily rag and polished the wing mirrors of a small Renault. If Libby wanted to know more, it appeared she'd have to ask Max.

13

'Where are you?'

'What?' The harsh trill of the phone broke into Libby's confused dream of sand, mud and dogs. 'What time is it?'

Marina exhaled loudly. 'It's half past one, and we're all here, waiting for you.'

Libby shook her head to click it into gear. 'I fell asleep.' She never fell asleep after lunch. She wished she'd kept Bear with her, instead of walking him back to Mrs Thomson's house. He would have kept her awake. 'I'm on my way.'

Her heart sank. Today, the local history society was giving a talk about Victorian women at Mangotsfield Hall, the huge mansion nearby, owned by the National Trust, and Marina was planning to demonstrate the clothes a Victorian lady wore. Libby had agreed to be a model chiefly because Trevor's ancestor had worked there as a maid, and Robert, her son, would love to see photos.

Unfortunately, the appointment had slipped her mind. 'You might have reminded me.'

'We talked about it on Tuesday.' Marina dropped the outraged voice. 'Look, don't panic. Angela's doing the magic lantern show first, so you've got a bit of time. I know how you feel, I've been all of a tizz ever since the Susie thing. Just get here as fast as you can.'

'What about refreshments?' Libby had planned to pick them up from the bakery.

'Mandy brought them over. She said she's staying with you? As a lodger?' The question hung in the air. No problem with Marina's gossip antennae.

Libby ignored it. 'Look, my car's in the garage. Can someone pick me up? I'll be ready in ten minutes.'

She grimaced. She'd agreed to some crazy things since she came to Exham, hoping to fit in with the townspeople, but it would probably take at least twenty years to be accepted as a local. She really ought to spend more time on her career. She was getting behind with the next book, and it was time she booked another cooking course. Baking. That was her future. And chocolate. She ran downstairs. Better not keep Marina waiting.

* * *

Marina's car screeched to a halt at the back of the Hall, at the tradesman's entrance. Libby dashed through another sudden downpour, frantically grasping the edges of an umbrella as the wind threatened to turn it inside out. She pasted a serene expression on her face as they walked in.

'It's OK.' Marina poked her head through a crack in the door. 'Angela's kept them busy.' Laughter blared from the hall, followed by applause as Angela finished.

'Come on, then,' Marina hissed. 'It's us next.' She gave her friend a hearty shove and Libby half fell into the hall.

She was never going to volunteer for anything, ever again. She really, really hated people staring. What had she been thinking?

Well, too late now. She smiled through clenched teeth, lips stiff, as Marina dressed her up in Victorian costume and make-up, beginning with a cotton shift and working up through layers of corsets and wire crinoline cages. She wouldn't be able to bear the weight for more than five minutes. How did Victorian ladies keep going all day?

Marina attached false ringlets to the sides of Libby's head. 'The Victorians thought it impolite for a lady to show her ears,' she explained, taking a pot of strong-smelling potion and a paint brush, and smoothing oil over Libby's hair. As it dried, Libby shook her head, but the ringlets stayed rigidly in place.

The result was a passable imitation of Queen Victoria. As though that were not sufficient humiliation, the audience gathered round, taking photos that threatened to haunt Libby for the rest of her life. They plucked at the costume, lifting heavy layers and letting them fall. 'Look, you can hardly raise your arms, those sleeves are so tight.'

'It's all part of the Victorian way of life,' Marina said. 'In fact, wearing a corset supports your back, don't you think, Libby,'

'I could wear this every day,' Libby lied. 'For one thing, it hides my waist. I could put on pounds and no one would notice.'

Slowly, the audience dispersed, chattering happily. At last, she could get rid of the costume and have a few words with Marina. 'What's in that disgusting stuff you spread all over my hair? You didn't warn me about that. How am I going to get it off?'

The words dried up on her lips as Libby caught sight of Detective Sergeant Joe Ramshore. She shifted, embarrassed. Did Joe know she'd been out to dinner with his father? Oh, well, who cared? She was a grown woman and Max was divorced. It was none of his son's business.

'Mrs Forest, I'm glad to see you.' Joe focused on Libby's hair and smirked. 'So sorry I missed the meeting. That costume looks terrific. And the hair...' He made a noise halfway between a laugh and a cough. 'Actually, I'm one of the trustees of Mangotsfield Hall and it's my day off today, but I'd like to have a word with you.'

Libby swallowed. Was she in trouble? About to be accused of obstructing the police by moving the body and taken into custody?

'Of course.'

'I wanted to tell you we've had the pathologist's report. It's no more than we expected. The cause of death was drowning while intoxicated. He found alcohol in Susie's blood. Probably not a deliberate overdose, just enough to stop Susie taking proper care around the water.'

'No sign of anything else?'

'A bruise on her head, but that would be the tide bashing her against the lighthouse. It was a rough old storm on Monday night.'

Libby tried to think. 'What about the time of death?'

'It's hard to tell. The body was in the water for a few hours, but it was so cold the pathologist can't tell when rigor mortis set in.' Libby winced. It was the stiffness of rigor mortis that had kept Susie's hand in her pocket, until Libby pulled it out to point at the sky.

'Look, Detective—'

'Call me Joe.' The grin told Libby he knew she'd been to dinner with his father.

'Look, aren't you going to investigate further? I mean, you said she was bruised. Don't you think that's suspicious? What if someone else was there?'

Joe sighed, looking suddenly tired. 'Please, Mrs Forest. We're grateful to you for calling us in as soon as you found the body, but now, you must leave it to us. We've seen hundreds of accidental deaths, you know, especially when there's drink or drugs involved.'

The patronising tone infuriated Libby. 'I know that, but common sense—'

'Common sense tells us there was nothing suspicious.' He'd raised his voice. 'Now, let me give you a bit of advice.' Joe's mouth smiled, but the eyes, as blue as his father's but ice cold, told a different story. Libby resisted a shiver.

'You're new here. You didn't know Susie. People feel strongly about her around here. They're proud. Not many from Exham end up famous. Folk don't like anyone suggesting she's more than just unlucky.' The blue gaze bored into Libby. 'We need to keep everyone calm. Talk a bit less about the drink and drugs, if you see what I mean. It was just an unfortunate accident.'

His tone was reasonable. 'Walking on the beach at this time of year is dangerous. The sea comes in fast. Susie's been away a long time and she forgot about the power of the tide.' He leaned towards Libby and spoke with emphasis. 'It was an accident, Mrs Forest. Leave it be. No more gossip.'

Gossip? That was rich. The whole town was abuzz with scandal. Libby shrugged. 'I didn't know her. I just found the body.' She hoped he hadn't heard details of her conversations with Max or her visit to Mrs Thomson.

'Exactly. You didn't know her. I'm just saying, some folks here don't take kindly to a stranger, who wasn't here in the old days, stirring things up.' His words silenced Libby. She tried to think of a sufficiently cutting reply, but before she could gather her wits, Joe walked away, leaving Libby, arms akimbo, mouth open.

Marina took her elbow. 'Are you OK?'

'I don't know. I think I've just been told to keep my nose out of town affairs.'

'By Detective Sergeant Joe?' Libby nodded. Marina waved a

hand. 'Don't worry about him. He can't get over his father coming back to town, just when Joe's been promoted to Chief Inspector's bagman. He wants to be top dog around here. You know, a big fish in a small pond. Max tends to cramp his style. It's family stuff.' She laughed. 'He's giving you a hard time because Max doesn't take enough notice of him.'

'Joe knows I've been out with Max,' Libby blurted.

Marina snorted. 'Of course he knows. It's the talk of the town, Libby. That's why the room was packed this afternoon. Everyone wanted to get a look at you.'

Libby's eyes threatened to pop out of her head. 'You mean, they're judging me?' She glanced over her shoulder. The few stragglers remaining in the hall stood in small knots, staring at her, fascinated. Libby choked back her anger, took a breath and stalked, fists clenched, eyes straight ahead, out through the door, as whispers chased close behind.

14

MANDY

The afternoon at Mangotsfield Hall had confirmed every one of Libby's fears about making a new life in a small town: gossip, cliques and the cold shoulder. London neighbours had warned her, but she'd thought she knew best. So much for those great plans for opening a chocolatier here. She was a laughing stock.

Safe at home, she grabbed a bottle of chardonnay from the fridge, filled a tall glass and took a satisfying gulp. As she drained the glass, and tilted the bottle again, ready for a top up, she caught sight of the clock. Mandy would be back soon, unless she'd changed her mind and found somewhere else to live or returned home.

Drinking wouldn't help. Libby had better cook dinner, instead.

She screwed the top back on the wine bottle, replaced it in the fridge and rifled through the shelves, looking for food. She had plenty of vegetables and some chicken. A stir fry, maybe? Something sharp and satisfying, with lovely noodles to warm the stomach.

Libby chopped and tasted, blending soy sauce with chili. She crushed garlic, relishing the sharp scent and the bite on her tongue, her spirits rising.

The door crashed open. Mandy appeared, soaked to the skin, tattooed arms full of flowers.

'These are for you.' The girl blushed crimson to the roots of the unnaturally black hair, plopped the flowers on the kitchen table, dropped a box of chocolates beside them, and walked out. 'For being kind.'

Libby heard the glue of tears in Mandy's voice as she disappeared upstairs.

Libby wiped her own, suddenly damp, eyes, ran cold water into a vase and cut the ends off the flower stems. She went to the foot of the stairs and shouted. 'Thanks. I love Alstroemeria.' She kept her voice matter of fact. 'They last for ages.'

Back in the kitchen, she turned on the radio, humming as she worked. A door closed upstairs and Mandy reappeared in dry clothes, wearing a sheepish grin. Libby longed to take a cloth to the girl's chalky face. Somewhere, under several inches of white make-up and lines of black kohl, hid a pretty face.

Libby reopened the wine, took out a clean glass and filled it, offering it to her new lodger. Mandy barely glanced at it before taking a long swig. Libby winced. Now wasn't the moment to pontificate about wine drinking, but it hurt to see good wine glugged like orange squash.

Mandy said, 'I heard about Joe Ramshore at the Hall.'

'News really does travel fast here, doesn't it?'

Mandy laughed. 'You said it. Anyway, don't take any notice of him. He's a fool. By the way, I told Mum I've officially left home, and you know what? She said, 'Good for you.'

'I'm sure she's glad. She worries about you. I know I—' Libby stopped. Mandy had enough problems without hearing a sob story about Libby's marriage. 'Mothers worry about their children.'

'Hmm. Maybe. Anyway, I told her to come over here if things get worse.'

Libby swallowed. 'Oh. Good idea.'

'Don't worry, she won't come. At least, I don't think so...'

Every scrap of dinner eaten, they lounged around in the sitting room, eating chocolate and watching television. Libby fiddled with kindling and firelighters until a blaze started in the fire. She rested twigs and bigger shards of wood on top in an elaborate cone shape.

'First fire of the year. Bet it goes out.'

The smell of apple wood scented the room. Libby breathed in, tension leaving her shoulders as she curled her feet up on the sofa. Fuzzy lay across Mandy's lap and purred loudly. 'She never sits with me,' Libby said. 'She likes you.'

Mandy dipped her head, cheeks reddening. 'Libby, I've been meaning to ask you something.'

'Ask away.'

'You said you're going to open a chocolate shop.'

Libby groaned. 'That's the idea. Sometimes it seems a very long way away. Don't tell Frank, because I don't want him to think I'm setting up in opposition to the bakery. I haven't decided yet. I've got a course coming up about the business side.' She wrinkled her nose. 'Not my favourite thing. Still, I don't want to be bankrupt in my first week. Then, I need to get more experience, and I've got to finish writing the next book, if I decide to do one. I haven't signed the contract yet.'

It sat on her computer, still waiting for a decision. 'Don't worry, Mrs Forest,' the publisher, a thin, exquisitely dressed young man, with a condescending attitude, had insisted. 'We'll do all the hard work for you. 'Baking at the Beach' was delightful, of course, but just a photo book, you know. Not – er – exactly professional. We're offering real expertise, and the chance for a bestseller.'

Libby had laughed.

'No, no, Mrs Forest – or, may I call you Libby – I mean it. We're one of the foremost publishers of creative crafts in the country. Of course, we can't offer an advance – but we'll bear all the organisation and all the costs.'

'And all I have to do is invent dozens of recipes, and test them?'

'Exactly. Oh, and provide a tiny story for each one – to keep the reader interested. Couldn't be easier.'

Libby told Mandy the story. 'So, we're looking at months, if not years, before I'll be in business for myself.'

'Well, when you do, I wondered—'

The phone rang. Libby, wishing she'd taken it off the hook, made a 'sorry' face at Mandy and answered. 'It's me. In Los Angeles.'

'Max. You're kidding. Really?'

'Really. I thought you'd want a progress report.'

'Report away.' She had things to say to Max when he got back, but they could wait.

He talked fast. 'I saw Susie's husband, Mickey. He's a jerk.'

'As we thought.'

'Quite. Well, he said, and I quote, he was sorry Susie was dead, but he hadn't seen her for years and he's far too busy with a new family to come to the funeral. He doesn't know what Susie was doing in Exham, and by the way, he wants to know if the will's been read yet. I suppose he's hoping to be in it.'

'Is there a will?'

'Your guess is as good as mine. Susie never mentioned it, but if she signed one, she might have left it with a solicitor.'

'What about the rest of her band? Did you track them down?'

'Mickey's assistant gave me addresses.' Libby heard a smile in his voice. 'Nice girl.' He'd have taken her out to dinner and pumped her for information. 'Guy the violinist and James the keyboard player left years ago and went back to England. The addresses may be out of date, but it's a start. I asked her if she knew about Susie's solicitor, but she didn't. Said Susie left all the business to Mickey. I'm heading back.'

'Back to Somerset? Not going to enjoy Los Angeles a while longer?'

He snorted. 'Alone in a hotel? Not my idea of fun. How are things?'

She paused. She wouldn't tell him about Joe. She didn't want to get involved in family jealousies. 'Fine.'

'Good. What about Mrs Thomson?'

'She showed me photos.'

The silence dragged on. 'Photos?'

'Of Annie Rose. Didn't Mickey mention her?'

'Who's Annie Rose?'

He didn't know? 'Mickey and Susie had a little girl who died when she was seven.'

The sharp intake of breath on the other end of the phone told Libby it was news to Max. 'Susie sent cards, and photos of her daughter to Mrs Thomson. Mickey didn't think to mention her?'

'I'm speechless. Look, I'll be home late on Saturday. Let's meet on Sunday: lunch at the Lighthouse Inn.'

'You'll be jet-lagged.'

'I've got through it before. A glass of pinot noir does the trick.'

Used to jet-setting around the world, then. Libby felt suddenly small and naïve. An afternoon in the local National Trust House, playing at dressing up, while Max flew halfway

around the world, probably club class. Bet he'd been everywhere.
'Libby?'

'Yes?'

'Thought we'd been cut off.'

'I was thinking. Can't you get back to Mickey and ask him about the little girl?'

'Tell you what. Email a copy of the little girl's photo for me to show him I mean business, and I'll try.'

Libby bit the inside of her cheek. She hadn't thought to ask for the photo, but she wasn't about to admit it. She'd have to nip back to Mrs Thomson's bungalow. She sighed. The car was in Jenkins' garage. 'I'm in the middle of something, I'll send it this evening.'

'OK. No hurry. Mickey won't go to bed at 9 o'clock, I bet. He'll be out on the town with his trophy wife. The secretary will tell me where he goes: I'm meeting her again at one of the bars here later today.'

Of course, you are. She couldn't resist you, could she?

'By the way. None of my business, but what exactly are you in the middle of?'

The cheek of the man. 'Mandy's here. You know, from the bakery? She's lodging with me. She came to-to...'

'To get away from her Dad?'

'Something like that.'

'OK. Good idea. He's a menace. Send the photo as soon as you can, Libby. See you on Sunday.'

Mandy appeared in the hall. Libby grabbed her keys. 'I'm popping out for a minute.'

'Can I come?'

Libby couldn't think of a reason to refuse. 'We'll have to walk.'

15

BREAKING AND ENTERING

'Mrs Thomson?' Libby rapped on the door. The light was on in the house and she could hear the TV. Mrs Thomson must have turned the sound up. Libby banged again, harder, and pressed the bell, keeping her thumb on the buzzer, but no one came.

Mandy spoke from behind Libby's shoulder. 'I'll go around the back.' She disappeared. Libby kept up the banging and ringing, but no one came. Where was Bear? He should be barking his head off by now.

Maybe Mrs Thomson had gone away. She might be visiting a friend, or a sister.

'Libby. Get help.' Mandy was back, panting. 'I looked through the window. I think she's had a fall.'

Libby dialled 999, hand shaking, remembering the last time she'd had to ring the police, on Tuesday. 'Fire, police or ambulance?'

'Ambulance. Police. Both.' Heart pounding, Libby ran with Mandy to the back of the house and peered through the kitchen window. The room gave nothing away: clean, neat and as tidy as before; plates stacked on the draining board; tea towels folded over the sink to dry. Mandy grabbed Libby's arm and pointed. The door to the hall stood ajar, and through the gap, Libby caught a flash of green. She groaned. Mrs Thomson's slippers. She'd been wearing them when Libby visited.

The door was locked. Libby shook it, but it held fast. She stood back, struggling to stay calm and sum up the problem. A pane of glass ran down the middle of the door. Libby gripped her phone in both hands and smashed it hard, into the panel. Broken shards clattered to the kitchen floor. She elbowed jagged fragments inwards, pulled the sleeve of her jacket down round her wrist, and slipped her arm through the door. The tips of her fingers touched the key. Grunting, she forced her shoulder further in, more splinters tinkling to the ground, until she could grasp the key between thumb and finger and turn it in the lock.

Praying Mrs Thomson hadn't shot the bolt across from the inside, Libby leaned on the handle. To her relief, the door swung open. She crunched across glass and pushed open the inner door. The old lady lay at the foot of the stairs, the back of her head angled against the wall. Mandy whispered. 'It looks as though her neck's broken.'

Another body. A wave of nausea struck Libby. She swallowed it down. No time for that, now. She felt Mrs Thomson's neck for a pulse, and fingered her wrist, horribly aware she'd done exactly the same for Susie.

'I think she's dead.'

Mandy's hand clamped to her mouth, muffling her voice. 'She must have fallen down the stairs.' She tugged Libby's elbow. 'Can't we do anything? Shouldn't we put a blanket over her, or something?'

'It's too late for that.' A news programme still blared from the television, echoing through the house. Libby's head pounded. She strode to the sitting room, found the remote control and switched off the set. Silence fell. A cup of tea, half finished, sat in its saucer on the table, next to one of Libby's walnut brownies. No steam rose from the cup. The tea must be cold. Libby knew better than to touch anything. Tears misted her eyes. Mrs Thomson had been alone, with no one nearby to help when she fell. Libby hoped she'd died instantly. The thought of the old lady lying in pain was unbearable.

The house was quiet: too quiet. What was wrong? *Bear.* Where was the dog? Why hadn't he barked when his mistress fell? A cold hand tugged at Libby's chest. She stepped with care around Mrs Thomson and set off up the stairs.

'Where are you going?' Mandy squeaked.

'The dog's missing.' Libby went through the house, opening one door after another. 'Bear, where are you? Come on out, it's me.'

Mandy sat on the stairs, transfixed by Mrs Thomson's body. 'Maybe he's outside?'

Before Libby could search the garden, horns blared, lights flashed, and the emergency services arrived in force. Joe Ramshore was first. 'Mrs Forest. What are you doing here?'

Mandy said. 'We found Mrs Thomson.'

'Did you?' He frowned at Libby, eyes narrowed, suspicious. The ambulance crew whispered in his ear. 'Another body,' he said. 'And once again, you're on the spot.' He took Libby's arm. 'Might I ask what you were doing here?'

* * *

The wooden chair at the police station, designed for utility rather than comfort, made Libby's back ache. She stared ahead at uninviting walls, bare of pictures or notices, painted dull grey. Mandy sat next to her at the plain wooden table, swirling cold, undrinkable tea inside a paper cup. Detective Sergeant Ramshore tilted his chair back, until only two legs touched the floor, waiting blank faced for an explanation.

'We went to the house to look at a photo,' she said. 'Mrs Thomson showed it to me earlier when I visited. To walk the dog.'

His expression didn't change. 'You were looking after Bear?'

'Max – your father – he's away.'

Joe raised one eyebrow in disbelief. 'And he asked you to take over the dog walking?'

Libby held his glance. 'Why not?'

He shrugged. 'So, you came back here in the evening, to visit an old woman? Didn't you realise you'd frighten her at this time of night? It looks like she tried to get to the door, wearing her ragged old slippers, and tripped on the stairs.'

'What?' Furious, Libby leaned forward. 'Are you saying it's my fault?'

'Have you got a better idea?'

'The dog's missing. Maybe she was going out to look for him?'

Joe crossed an ankle over the other leg, tapping his cup with a long finger. 'In the dark? We'd know more about that if you hadn't broken in, making such a mess of the back door, wouldn't we?'

'We had to get in.' Libby was indignant. 'We could see her at the bottom of the stairs. She could still have been alive?'

'OK.' He uncrossed his legs. 'Fair enough, I suppose. Anyway, I'm afraid the poor old soul's gone. She must have been almost ninety, and she lived all on her own. Something like this was bound to happen one day.'

'You think it's another accident, then?'

The detective laughed. 'Mrs Forest, please don't start imagining someone murdered Mrs Thomson. Old ladies fall all the time. It's amazing she lasted so long, alone in this place. No one broke in. The only damage is to the kitchen door, thanks to you.'

'Can we go home, then?'

When Joe smiled, he looked like his father. 'I'll get one of my men to drive you.' Tired, Libby and Mandy trudged along the drab corridor of the police station. 'And Mrs Forest.'

She stopped. 'Yes?'

'Try not to find any more bodies for a few days.'

16

BEAR'S ADVENTURE

Libby tapped out a brief text for Max before she fell, exhausted, into bed.

Can't send photo after all. Explain later. Please text addresses of band members

She was asleep even before the whooshing noise sounded, announcing that the text had gone.

A series of messages greeted her when she woke.

What's going on?
Hope everything OK.
Here are addresses

She smiled. Max was no more able to use text speak, full of gr8 and thx, than she. She copied the addresses onto a scrap of paper and folded it, sliding it into a pocket in her handbag.

'I'm worried about Bear.' She poured cornflakes into a bowl. Mandy, white faced, a faded grey dressing gown pulled up to her chin, looked like a vampire. She cradled a coffee cup in both hands and grunted. Libby hid a smile. It was good to have a teenager about the place again, failing to communicate. 'I'm going back to see what happened.'

'You know it's not half past six yet, don't you?'

'You can talk.' Concerned, Libby considered Mandy's pale face. 'Couldn't you sleep?'

Mandy shivered. 'I kept thinking about that poor old lady.'

'I know. We'll talk about it later, after you get back from the bakery. In the meantime, I'm going to find out what happened to Bear.'

I can't face Max if something happens to the dog, as well as to Mrs Thomson. She longed to email or ring, to tell him, but she couldn't. It would be unfair while he was too far away to help.

Fiercely, she chopped a banana into tiny pieces and dropped them into her bowl. 'I can't just leave him any longer.' Besides, she wanted to get to the Thomson house early. There was a job she meant to do.

Mandy heaved a sigh and pushed herself up from the table. 'I'll come with you.'

'No.' She wouldn't involve Mandy any further. 'You have to get to the bakery. I landed you in enough trouble yesterday, and I won't do it again. If Detective Sergeant Ramshore finds out we've been back to the crime scene, we'll go straight to the top of the suspect list. That is, when he works out Mrs Thomson didn't fall.'

Mandy's mouth hung open. 'You think she was pushed?'

'Of course she was. How many unexplained sudden deaths does a place like Exham have in the average week? Yet, here are two in a few days.'

Mandy sucked at a corner of toast. 'There are lots of old people here. You know, in Haven House and that new place near the kid's playground. There must be dozens of people dying every week.'

'I hope you're exaggerating. Anyway, Susie wasn't old and it's too much of a coincidence.' Libby stirred the banana into her cereal. 'Think about it. She comes back to Exham for some reason, we don't know why. Next minute, she's dead. Then, one of the few people who really cared about her dies.'

She pointed her spoon at Mandy. 'I was beginning to think the police were right, and Susie's death was an accident, but this is one coincidence too many.'

Mandy got to her feet and stacked her bowl in the dishwasher. 'In that case, I'll definitely come with you. You can't go alone. Someone has to keep you out of trouble.'

Libby choked on her cornflakes. 'Nonsense. I'll be careful. Anyway, Frank can't bake bread and serve at the same time, and we mustn't let him down.'

If she hadn't been so worried about Bear, Libby would have enjoyed the walk to Mrs Thomson's house. The wind had died away overnight, and the rain had stopped. The sun was almost up, peeping from between heavy clouds that threatened more storms before long. She'd offer to take Shipley out soon. She'd been neglecting him, deserting the poor animal for Bear, and she doubted Marina would have exercised him.

They'd have a good run on the beach later, before the weather broke again.

As expected, the police had boarded up Mrs Thomson's back door. Libby walked on, out into the half acre garden. The late Mr Thomson's retirement pride and joy looked neglected, the pond clogged with duckweed and dead leaves. A few remnants of foliage clung to grey overhanging branches. Beds of roses had run to a riot of hips and haws. Something for the birds to enjoy, at least.

Libby called softly. 'Bear?' No answer. She called again and whistled. What was that? She strained her ears. The sound had come from her right, where a sturdy shed nestled against a ragged yew hedge. Libby tugged at the door until it creaked open. Bear sprawled in the corner. He raised his massive head, staggered to his feet, whined, wobbled and lay down again.

Libby's stomach heaved as she caught the acrid scent of sick. A pool of vomit stank nearby. Fresh scratches covered the shed door, where the dog had tried to get out. Bear whined again, and lay, head on paws, exhausted.

'What happened to you, Bear?'

The shed was clean and warm, and a selection of doggy toys suggested Bear sometimes slept there. His basket was lined with old sweaters, positioned close to an empty bowl. Judging by the nearby splashes, it had recently held water. Another bowl held a lump of meat, half eaten. Bear had only taken a bite or two.

Libby rubbed her knuckles against the top of his bony head and the dog nuzzled her hand. 'What did they give you? You seem to be on the mend, old thing. I'll take you home with me and look after you today.' She straightened up. 'But first, I need to get into the house.' There was a toolbox in the shed. This was going to be easier than she'd thought.

The lock on the back door was still broken. The police had nailed hardboard roughly across the opening, half to the door, the rest attached to the frame. She'd better be quick. A locksmith would probably arrive this morning, to secure the house properly.

She opened the toolbox, glanced round to check she was alone, grasped the biggest hammer firmly, hooked the claw behind the first nail and twisted. The nail popped out. So did the second. The third was awkward, bending and sticking, and

Libby's hair was stuck to her head with sweat by the time she wrenched it out.

As she levered out the fourth and final nail, the door swung open and she stepped inside. The broken glass had been swept away. She tiptoed into the front room, stopped and straightened. No need to tread with such care; there was no one in the house to hear her. She let her gaze rove across the crowded tables and shelves. Nothing had changed since she'd been here with Mrs Thomson.

The old lady's presence seemed to fill the air. Libby shivered and whispered, 'I hope they didn't scare you, before they shoved you down the stairs.' How exactly had she died? Libby's head spun with different scenarios. Maybe they took Mrs Thomson by surprise, and she died, mercifully, hardly knowing what happened. Or perhaps the killer was someone Mrs Thomson knew and trusted. Lonely, she might have let them in, just as she'd welcomed Libby.

Libby doubted that. Mrs Thomson had said she never answered the door after six.

'I won't mess up your house, I promise. I just need those photographs.' Libby spoke out loud, as though the old lady could hear her.

The album lay where she'd last seen it, among a pile of notebooks and scraps of paper.

'I'll find out who killed Suzanne,' Libby added.

She started to flick through the stack of papers, fingers fumbling. Her head flew up. What was that noise? Someone was outside.

She grabbed the pile of papers and books, along with the album, and thrust them all into her shoulder bag. Just in time. The door flew open.

'What the—' Detective Sergeant Ramshore slid to a halt,

halfway between Libby and the door, arms folded. 'Mrs Forest. I might have known. This is breaking and entering, you know.'

Libby thought fast. 'I'm worried about the dog. I came back to find him.'

Joe hooked his thumbs into his belt. 'Well, one of my men found him in the shed. Looks like he slept there last night, so you can go home again, Mrs Forest, and please, please, just stay away.'

'I was going to take him home with me, if he's well enough.'

Joe's face cleared. 'Good idea. Make yourself useful. And don't come back.' He stood aside and Libby slipped past, making light of the heavy shoulder bag, hoping he wouldn't ask to see inside it. Sometimes, age and gender had its uses. He'd have spent longer talking to a pretty young girl, and he'd have been suspicious of a man, but a woman of a certain age, old enough to be his mother…

Maybe he'd decided Libby was just a foolish, interfering older woman. She bit her lip to keep a tell-tale smile from her face.

'Wait.' Joe held up a hand. Libby stopped, heart racing. She'd celebrated too soon. Was he about to search the bag? She'd have a job explaining the stack of stolen papers. 'I've got some news. I suppose you're entitled to hear it first, as you found her.'

'About Mrs Thomson?' Libby stood sideways, her bag clasped under the arm furthest away from the officer, her body shielding it from view.

'No, about Susie Bennett. The complete postmortem shows more bruising than we thought: more than the pathologist thinks would result from being thrown about in a storm.'

'Bruising? What does that mean?' No harm in continuing to play the innocent woman.

'It means you may be right, crazy as it sounds. Susie Bennett might, just possibly, have been murdered.'

'Do you – do you know who did it?'

He leaned back against the wall, legs set apart, every inch the bold investigator. 'Not yet. I'll be surprised if we ever find out. A body on the beach, in a storm. No evidence, you see. Still, don't leave town, Mrs Forest.'

Libby slipped out of the room, clutching the bag tight to her body.

Joe had already lost interest in her. 'Better get the door fixed right now, Evans, before the rest of the town comes to visit.'

By the time she arrived home, Bear trooping, listless, beside her, Libby's shoulder ached from the weight of books. Her mind raced. As she'd turned to leave Mrs Thomson's sitting room, she'd glanced out of the window. From there, the widow could see right along the beach, to the pier on the left and the lighthouse to the right.

What if Mrs Thomson had stood, looking out into the storm, on Monday night? She might have seen something unusual. More than the storm and high tide. Something that had got her killed.

17

GUY

The faithful old Citroen was due for collection today. Libby checked the time. Yes, if she hurried, she could pick up the car and visit both of Susie's band members today.

Bear recovered fast, growing perkier every moment until he bounded up and down the hall with his usual vigour. How long could Libby keep a dog his size in this tiny cottage?

Oh, well, she'd worry about that later. Meanwhile, she dug out an ancient apple crate from the cupboard under the stairs, dragged it into a warm spot in the hall and lined it with old blankets. 'There you are, my lad.' She took a step into the sitting room and held her breath. Fuzzy lay curled by the door, in one of her favourite spots where hot water pipes lay under the floor.

Bear heaved himself to his feet, looming over the cat, panting.

Was Libby about to witness an epic fight? She grabbed Bear's collar. Fuzzy stood, yawned and stretched her back legs.

Then, to Libby's amazement, the cat began to purr. Libby dropped her hold on Bear. 'When did you two make friends?'

The dog leaned over, touched his nose to Fuzzy, and settled down next to his new buddy.

Libby stashed Mrs Thomson's photo album in a drawer and walked to the garage. She'd spend the evening poring through the book for clues.

Alan Jenkins wiped oily hands on a blue overall. 'Ah. Mrs Forest, there you are. She's just about ready for you.' Why did men always call cars, 'she'?

He still insisted on refusing payment. 'Tell Max it's a present.' He'd even topped the Citroen up with petrol. Was Max some kind of Godfather around here?

Tired of arguing, Libby held out a packet of her homemade shortbread. Alan's eyes lit up.

'You're a good woman.' What was it the old wives used to say about the way to a man's heart being through his stomach?

The road to Bath twisted through tiny villages, along a road too narrow for more than one car. Marina told her it was quicker by train, but Libby needed her own transport. She'd made up her mind to visit both the other members of Susie's old, defunct band, before Max returned. James, the keyboard player, lived just outside Bristol, and Guy, the violinist, lived in Bath.

She'd thrown a ham salad into a Tupperware container before setting off, and she pulled over beside the Chew Valley Lake, to eat. She took a bite and screwed up her nose. The dressing didn't taste quite right. Maybe a little too much lemon juice? Or not enough honey? She'd make up another batch soon.

It was days since she'd had time to potter around in the kitchen, experimenting. Once this business was over, she planned to lock herself in for hours and get on with devising recipes. Before long, she'd have to give Niles Fisher, the publisher, her answer about the book.

Libby felt a twinge inside at the thought. She planned a series of excuses as she ate, opening the door to let a few rays of sunshine warm her. *Dead bodies: that would do it.* At least it had the advantage of being true, and Mr Fisher had no way of knowing the bodies in question were unrelated to Libby.

She threw a crust of bread into the water. Excited ducks scrambled over one another. Libby took out a chunk of sultana cake. The ducks wouldn't get any of this, her favourite comfort food.

Every last crumb eaten, she climbed back into the car, crunching gears in sudden excitement. Maybe Susie's old band-mate, Guy, would have some answers.

His double-fronted Georgian house stood, white-painted, in a block of similar graceful homes. To Libby's surprise, the door flew open almost before she'd had time to drop the brass lion-head knocker, as if he'd been expecting her.

The man's appearance took her aback. She'd been prepared for aging hippy long hair, flares or a tasselled waistcoat. Instead, his short, neat haircut, shirt, and the final touch, a silk tie with a Windsor knot, were conventional enough to have pleased Libby's parents. He was only a short step away from a cardigan.

His lined face wore the slightly anxious look of a middle-aged man whose mirror proves his youth is disappearing fast. He led her inside.

'Max rang to say you'd be coming.'

So, it was Max who gave the game away. Annoying man. Libby had lost the element of surprise.

'Anyway,' Guy shrugged. 'Susie was all over the local news. I thought I'd hear something from Exham. When's the funeral?

Was the man upset? Libby couldn't tell. The pupils of his eyes were big and dark. He pushed wire-rimmed glasses further up a long nose and waved at a selection of wines and spirits on a breakfast bar.

'We don't have a date yet. Not until after the inquest.'

Guy nodded. 'I'd like to be there for Susie. We had some good times together in the old days. Drink?'

The huge, airy kitchen was clean and, unlike Guy himself, at the cutting edge of modern design. Libby flicked her gaze round the room, finding no sign of a wife or children among the uncompromising shine of black granite and glassy smooth white paint.

She shook her head. 'I'm driving, but I'd love a coffee.'

'Ah. Good choice.' Guy clattered around the huge, gleaming chrome of the coffee machine with milk jugs and coffee. Libby hid a smile. Kenco and hot water would have taken half the time.

The coffee, when at last it arrived, was perfect. 'So, you found Susie on the beach. That's sad. Not quite the dramatic end I'd expect of her. She'd have preferred something outrageous, like a mistimed bungee jump.' When Guy smiled, he showed beautiful white teeth. They must be the result of the band's success in America. 'Was it the drink that killed her?'

There was no reason to hide the truth. 'In fact, she had been drinking, but I'm afraid it looks like murder.'

That caught the man's attention. He blinked. 'Seriously?'

Libby pressed on, glad to have dented his calm surface. Now, maybe he'd forget any prepared speeches. 'There are a few suspects. I imagine the police will visit you, soon.'

A flash of consciousness, a widening of the eyes, told Libby she'd hit a nerve. He shot a glance around the kitchen, and she realised what had seemed odd about him. His gaze unfocused, his eyes dark, his behaviour too casual.

The man was stoned. Libby wondered where he kept the drugs.

'Excuse me.' He stepped outside the kitchen, into the hall, and called up the stairs. 'Alvin?'

'Yeah. What is it?' A younger man, in his twenties, hair longer, mussed up, his sleeveless t-shirt showing muscled arms, leaned over the banister.

'Clean things up, will you?'

The younger man frowned, puzzled for a moment, then his brow cleared. 'Right. OK.'

Libby gulped down the coffee. She had to get her questions out before Guy cut the conversation short. He'd want time to clear the house of incriminating drug paraphernalia.

'I just want to find out about Susie. What happened after all those albums, when she came back to Exham, and why? Those sorts of things.'

He shrugged. 'Don't ask me. Didn't know she was here. The band broke up years ago, and we all lost touch. We made a bit of money. I had enough to buy this place.' He looked around the kitchen, beaming. 'Bought a house for my mother, as well. She's in a care home, now, but she had a good few years.'

'What about Susie's marriage?'

The smile faded. He shrugged. 'Usual showbiz thing. Mickey found a newer, younger model. You know – longer legs, blonder hair. Anyway, Susie lost her spark when...'

He stopped, licked his lips and shot a sideways glance at Libby. She let the pause go on as she rinsed her cup and dried it, but Guy offered no more details.

She'd have to prompt. 'OK. I know about the little girl that died. Annie.'

'Annie Rose, yeah. Cute little thing.' The lines on Guy's face softened. Libby glimpsed a warmer, kinder man somewhere under the surface. 'Broke Susie's heart when little Annie died.'

'And Mickey's too?'

'What? Oh, yeah, of course. He was upset. We all were. That's when Susie said she couldn't go on. We tried to talk her out of it, but who could blame her? Something like that cuts you right up.

She left LA, went up north, heading for Canada. She had some sort of connections there; distant family, or something. She was a bit vague.'

'Has she been in touch?'

'Nope. Clean break. I came back to Bath, took an OU course in computing.'

Libby laughed. 'Computing? After life in a band?'

He pushed his glasses up again. 'Well, I'd always done the techie stuff. I played violin a bit, sure, but I preferred to tinker with the sound system.' He shrugged again. 'Not really cut out for travelling. It was good to get off the road and settle down.'

'Apart from the drugs.'

He shuffled his feet. 'Just weed. Nothing heavy.'

'Anything else you can tell me about Susie?'

'She was a nice kid. If I'd known she was in England I'd have got in touch.'

Alvin shambled into the kitchen, scratching at an unshaven chin, and Libby beat a retreat. Guy seemed to know as little about Susie as her old school mates in Exham. It was as though she'd been a ghost, passing through people's lives.

One question above all others hammered in Libby's head. What on earth had Susie been doing in Exham after all those years away?

18

Libby fiddled with the Satnav, planning the route to Weldon on the other side of Bristol, aware that someone, either Guy or Alvin, was watching from a window. They wanted to make sure she'd left the area. She revved the engine and wound down the window, waving with enthusiasm. She'd have time to visit Susie's other band mate if she set off now.

The route to James Sutcliffe's home took Libby down a series of ever more winding, narrow roads. She stopped to check her iPhone. Surely no one lived down this tiny, overgrown lane, hedges high on either side?

No signal. Should she give up, reverse back and go home? A horn blared and Libby twisted in her seat. She flinched. A monster tractor filled the whole of the rear window. The engine ground to a halt at the last moment, inches away.

The driver dragged off a pair of headphones, swung down from the cab, and rolled across to her window. A knitted jumper of indeterminate colour lay, unravelling, over his paunch. His head was stubbly and weathered. He shoved a ruddy, belligerent face close to the glass. 'Where you off to, then?

He'd left Libby no space to open the Citroen's door. Trapped and furious, she lowered the window and used her iciest voice. 'What business is it of yours?'

'If you're on the way to Ross on Wye, you need to go back, turn right onto the main road, and take the motorway. And don't use that Satnav. Can't be trusted.'

'How can I reverse with your tractor practically in my back seat? Anyway,' she remembered why she was here. 'I'm looking for James Sutcliffe. I think he lives nearby.'

'Ah.' The eyes narrowed. 'Huh. Plenty like you come up here on the way to Ross. No more sense than the day they're born. Buy an expensive Satnav, throw away perfectly good maps and get lost here, in my lane. You're going nowhere this way, let me tell you.'

Libby picked out information from an apparently well-practised rant. 'Your lane? You must be Mr Sutcliffe.'

'So, who wants me?' Must they have the conversation here? Libby peered ahead, but she couldn't see around the corner. The cultured voice of the Satnav recovered and broke in, insisting that in one hundred yards she would reach her destination.

Libby pulled out the connection. 'I want to ask about Susie Bennett.'

'Thought so.' James Sutcliffe was triumphant. The colour in his cheeks, previously the sort of dull pink a kind observer would describe as a healthy, open air glow, darkened to purple. Was he about to have a stroke? At least that would stop him blowing Libby's head off with a shotgun. 'Just get off my land, woman. I've had enough of journalists nosing into my business.'

'No, no, I'm not a journalist.' The squeak in Libby's voice was less than convincing.

'Who says so?' The man had a good point. It was one thing to prove you were something: journalists carried ID cards, didn't they, like police officers? Much harder to prove you were nothing special, just a normal person. Not that Libby felt very normal, given the events of the past few days.

She slapped on what she hoped was a non-journalistic smile, aiming for a mix of seriousness and reason. 'Anyway, even if I came from a newspaper, I can't go back until you move your tractor.'

Sutcliffe growled. 'Get yourself up to the yard.' He stomped back to the tractor.

The vast front end was only inches from her car. Libby feared for the newly repaired Citroen. She clashed gears and cursed under her breath, and the car lurched further up the lane, finally rounding the corner to rest on a cobbled farmyard.

Mud, an inch thick, covered uneven cobbles. Libby groaned. She'd chosen her shoes with care: elegant red patent with kitten heels and elaborate holes cut into the sides. Wholly appropriate for the refined ambience of Georgian Bath, they were unlikely to survive an encounter with farmyard muck. The temptation to wheel round and disappear back up the lane was almost overwhelming.

Holding the door for support, feet slithering, she edged out of the car. 'Mr Sutcliffe, I'm honestly not from the media. I've just been talking to Guy. Guy Miles.' The farmer frowned, obviously recognising the name. Libby held out her phone. 'Ring him, if you like.'

Libby had never heard anyone harrumph before, but that was what Sutcliffe did. He brushed past the outstretched phone. 'Better come in, then.'

She ducked under a low doorway that opened into a huge kitchen. Mud from the yard had infiltrated, using the convenient transport of Sutcliffe's boots, through the ill-fitting door. It carpeted the otherwise bare, flagstone floor of a rustic room, apparently undecorated since the 1950s. Rickety orange boxes, stacked underneath and to the side of a huge, pine table, teetered and trembled. Libby caught a glimpse of greaseproof paper and a logo showing a goat's head. Sutcliffe, proving himself to be no more of a talker indoors than in the lane, uttered one word. 'Cheese.'

19

CHEESE

'Dairy's over there.' He pointed through the window. To be sure, behind the run-down farmhouse nestled a contrasting complex of neat brick buildings, doors and windows smart with red paint, enclosing a small yard lined with pristine paving stones. In the distance, a herd of goats tugged up mouthfuls of grass in a paddock, as though on a mission. 'Jack runs the business now.'

The unexpected burst of information brought Libby back to the filthy kitchen. Could that be pride in the farmer's voice?

'Jack?' She guessed. 'Your son?'

'Ah. Lives over yonder with that fancy wife of his.' Sutcliffe's ruddy face had calmed. Social relations had somehow been restored. The farmer gestured towards a battered brown kettle. 'Tea?'

'Yes, please. Let me get the cups.' Many more of these visits and she'd float away on a tide of tea and coffee. She pulled mugs from the wobbling pile on the draining board and seized the opportunity to inspect them for grime. She'd seen worse.

Sutcliffe fiddled with kettle and tea caddy. Libby coughed.

'Susie Bennett. You were in the band, with her and Guy, isn't that right?'

'Ah.' Sutcliffe kept his back turned.

'I found her body.'

He stopped, kettle poised inches above an ancient, cracked teapot. His words were almost inaudible. 'Did you now? All alone on the beach?'

The bluster drained away from the red face, leaving it crumpled, like a crushed eggshell. Libby took the kettle, pouring hot water into the pot, giving the farmer time to blow a loud nasal blast on a grubby handkerchief. 'Little Susie. Who'd have thought it?'

The door opened and a younger, taller, cleaner version of James Sutcliffe strode in. Any hope the son would prove more welcoming than his father evaporated. He threw a cursory glance at Libby. 'What's going on, here, Dad?'

Sutcliffe wiped his eyes. Libby assessed the distance to the door, wishing she could just leave, annoyed to have misread James Sutcliffe. The gruff exterior hid deep feelings.

'I – I'm sorry.' Lost for adequate words, she sniffed a nearby bottle of milk, decided there was life left in it, and poured three cups of tea. 'I came to find out more about Susie Bennett.'

'You've picked a bad time.' The son pulled out a wooden chair and his father sank into it. 'Dad's wife died a month ago. The news about Susie just about finished him off.'

Libby gulped. No wonder the place was such a mess. James Sutcliffe had been running on empty, trying to keep going after the tragedy.

A thought struck. Jack Sutcliffe had said, 'Dad's wife.' She wasn't his own mother then.

He folded his arms. 'What's it all to do with you, anyway?'

'I found Susie's body. On the beach, under the lighthouse. I just wanted to find out more about her. The police aren't interested, but she'd been away for so long...'

'The lighthouse?' James Sutcliffe interrupted. 'That's where we used to do our courting, back along when we were lads. Bonfires on the beach, hanky-panky in the dunes.' Libby studied the rugged face, searching for a likeness to the youth in the photograph. Life had been hard for Susie's old friend.

Jack opened a series of tins, peered into one and offered it to Libby. 'Rich tea?'

She took one, dunking it in her mug. 'I just wanted to find out why Susie was back in England. I thought her old band mates might know.'

The older Sutcliffe stuffed his handkerchief in a pocket, packed a biscuit into his mouth and mumbled. 'Came to see my Mary.'

His son translated. 'Susie wanted to see my stepmother before she died. It was cancer. It took a long time for her to go.'

Libby sat back. The answer to Susie's presence in the area was as simple as that: no mystery, after all. Susie had come back to visit old friends in trouble. 'I'm very sorry for your loss.'

Sutcliffe's son filled in the details. James married his first wife in the United States before the band broke up. The marriage didn't last long: the first Mrs Sutcliffe had a sharper eye for business than for romance and left her husband and young son for a wrinkled but rich American tycoon. Susie stayed in touch when the newly divorced James brought his son, Jack, home to the UK and turned to farming.

'She used to write, now and then.' Jack smiled. 'Even sent me presents from America. T-shirts and sneakers: things you couldn't get in England, then. Like an aunt, really.'

'Do you have any letters?'

Sutcliffe shrugged. 'Threw them away. Anyway, they were

private.' Libby held up a hand. 'I'm not being nosy, Mr Sutcliffe. You see, no one knows exactly what happened. How Susie died, I mean. It seemed like she'd been drinking and got caught in the high tide.'

Sutcliffe snorted. 'Susie wouldn't get caught. She grew up in Exham. Knew every inch of the beach. She'd never let the tide catch her like one of those summer visitors. She drank like a fish, mind you, that's true enough.'

Libby smiled. 'You must have known her daughter?' She looked from one man to the other. 'I heard Annie Rose drowned.'

Sutcliffe clenched his fists and hammered them on the table, rattling the mugs. 'If I could get my hands on that man...' He pointed a finger at Libby. 'Neglect. That's what killed Susie's little girl. Mickey Garston let her die because he was too lazy to look after her.'

'Dad.' Jack intervened, one hand on his father's arm. 'No one really knows what happened. Anyway, that was years ago. It's Susie's death we're talking about. You're saying it might have been an accident?'

Libby shrugged. 'No. Murder.' She let that thought sink in.

Sutcliffe clattered the mugs together and threw them in the sink. 'Mickey Garston. That's who's behind it, you mark my words. Susie cursed the day she met that man. Just let me get at him...' Jack laid a hand on his father's shoulder, but the older man shrugged it off. 'Should have dealt with him myself, years ago.'

'Mickey was in America when she died,' Libby said. 'Besides, why would he want her dead after so many years?'

'I'll show you.' Sutcliffe left the room. Libby heard drawers opening, papers being shuffled. 'Here it is.' He held out two pages of writing paper. He hadn't thrown all her letters away then.

Libby glanced at the signature. *Love, Susie, xxx.* She read through the childish script.

Dear Jamie and Mary,

Thank you for the beautiful flowers you sent, and for remembering the anniversary of Annie Rose's death. She would have been ten years old. I still can't believe she's gone.

I miss England very much, but I won't come back. I have friends out here and the sun always shines. Most important, though, is I can visit Annie Rose's grave to talk to her.

You probably heard Mickey and I split up. It's been all over the news programmes. He's going to divorce me. I'd stop it, if I could, but Californian law won't let me. It makes me angry. Why should I set him free to marry someone else, after all he's done? My mistake was marrying him in the first place.

I want him to be miserable…

Libby re-read the letter. 'Divorce?' She let the idea take root in her brain. 'So, Mickey was her ex-husband. And now, Mickey's married to another woman.'

She thought for a moment. 'I wonder if Susie named Mickey in her will, or if she made another after the divorce?'

Sutcliffe rocked his chair back. 'Susie wouldn't let Mickey know how much money she had. I bet she put it somewhere out of his reach.'

Libby was still thinking it through. 'I don't blame her. She wouldn't want to rely on Mickey for alimony.'

Sutcliffe laughed; the sound sharp as a whip crack. 'You have to understand Susie, you see. Most people don't. At school, she was a bit of an outcast, because her parents were travellers. Her mother came from an old gypsy family. As for her dad, he was long gone when she was just a bairn.'

'Susie's parents never bothered to get married. No one knows what happened to her old man: he'll have died, long ago. Travellers live free as air, but they don't live long. Her Ma died while we were in the States.'

'Our Susie was more of a gypsy than anyone I've ever met. She didn't care about money. She did things the traveller's way: with a handshake. I'd be willing to bet my farm she died without leaving a will. Probably didn't even have a solicitor.'

'That means Susie's money...'

Sutcliffe slapped the table with one hand. 'It means Mickey might think he can get his hands on Susie's fortune – but he can't. It'll go to her family, no matter how distantly they're related.'

MUSHROOM SAUCE

Libby's bones ached as she turned into the lane leading to Hope Cottage in the dark. She longed to get home, close the curtains to shut out the world, light the sitting room with the gentle glow of table lamps, collapse onto the comfortable sofa and think.

If only Max were here, she could run today's discoveries past him. Had he found out any more about Mickey? Susie's husband had an alibi, but that didn't mean he couldn't mastermind Susie's death from the other side of the Atlantic. It all depended on Susie's will.

She yawned and drove onto the drive. She'd hardly had time to think about Mrs Thomson's fall. Had the old lady been pushed: killed for something she'd seen through the wind and rain of Monday night? Libby shivered. Two women were dead, and the local police weren't bothering to investigate. She felt very alone. If she didn't persist, Susie and Mrs Thomson would be forgotten.

Later, she'd look through the photos in the old lady's album. Who knew what else she might uncover from Susie's past? But first, she needed a large glass of wine. Her mouth watered in anticipation as she parked the car in the drive, fumbled in her bag for keys, and unlocked the door.

As it opened, a wave of noise erupted. Mandy, the Goth. Libby had forgotten all about her. Televisions blared from every downstairs room. Above the racket, Mandy was singing, tuneless but enthusiastic. Libby shouted. 'Mandy.' She waited. 'Mandy.' She clattered up the stairs to hammer on the door of Mandy's room.

The door swung open. 'Oh, hello, Libby.' Mandy, eyes wide, covered her mouth with one hand and pulled an earphone off one ear. 'Sorry, am I too noisy? Mum thumps on the ceiling with a broom handle when she wants me to shut up.'

Libby's exasperation dissolved. Having Mandy around reminded her of the recent, bitter-sweet days, when her own noisy teenagers lived with her, shoes and bags littering the hallway, damp towels everywhere and the fridge emptied as fast as she filled it. The angry retort died on her lips. 'Is chicken and chips OK for dinner?'

'Wow, wonderful. With some of that special sauce you told me about?'

'Ready in half an hour.'

Bear and Fuzzy were still snoring in the sitting room. The dog had needed to recover and Fuzzy, over ten years old, could snooze for at least three quarters of every day, waking only to eat and wander outside hoping in vain to catch a bird.

Bear woke as she entered the room. 'You can sleep through Mandy's racket, but you hear me come in on stockinged feet?' Dogs, Libby decided, were remarkable creatures.

Leaving the animals, Libby opened a bottle of pinot noir in the kitchen. Mandy was lodging permanently so it was time to wean her off sweet white fizz. Forgetting the tired ache in her back, Libby set about preparations with enthusiasm. She made salad dressing, sliced potatoes into chips, washed vegetables and fried a handful of chestnut mushrooms in olive oil. In a minute or two, she'd add some crushed garlic, a slug of brandy, a whisk of mustard and a dollop of cream, and the sauce would be perfect.

She breathed in garlic and olive oil, the scent of sunshine and happiness. Mandy burst into the kitchen. 'Mm. Smells good.'

Libby handed over a glass, one third full. 'Sit down, Mandy. You're not to take a single mouthful yet.'

'What? Why not?'

'You'll enjoy it more, this way. Trust me.' Mandy rolled her eyes, but waited, glass in hand. 'Now, just circle the glass in your hand, so the air gets at the wine. That's it. Be gentle,' as Mandy's wine threatened to spill over the top of the glass. 'Now, have a look at the colour. Gorgeous, isn't it? OK, now get your nose in the glass and sniff.'

Mandy giggled and put on a fake, affected wine tasting voice. 'I'm getting peaches, brambles and a spot of manure.' Libby threw a tea towel at her. 'Maybe I need another glass to be sure.'

'Wait a minute, here's the food.'

Libby served the chicken breasts. Mandy spooned salad from the oversized wooden bowl onto her plate. 'Mmm. Scrumptious.'

'Had a good day at the shop?'

'Your latest recipe went down well. What about your day? Made any discoveries?'

'Not about Mrs Thomson, I'm afraid, but I found out one or two things about Susie.'

Mandy's phone rang. She bit her lip. 'It's Mum.' She pressed the button and her voice rose. 'Calm down, Mum, I can't hear you.'

Libby could hear Elaine's voice on the other end of the phone. It sounded scared. Mandy's hand shook as she covered the phone to hiss at Libby. 'It's Dad. He's having one of his tempers – stomping around upstairs and shouting.'

'Tell your Mum to come over here. She mustn't stay there. No, wait, I'll go and get her.'

Mandy relayed the message to her hysterical mother. 'No, Mum, stay there, but keep an eye out. Libby's coming.' Her voice rose. 'Mum, I can hear him. Get out of the house, now!'

Libby ran to the car and accelerated away, tyres screaming. The drive took less than three minutes. She screeched to a halt, just as Mandy's mother, coat-less despite the cold, ran out, fumbling at the car door. Libby leaned over to release the catch and Elaine half fell into the car, shivering, cheeks wet with tears, teeth chattering so she could barely speak. 'I s-sneaked out the back door when Bert went to get b-beer from the fridge.'

Bert burst through the front door, bottle raised, and Elaine screamed. Libby stepped on the accelerator.

'Hold tight.' The Citroen roared away from the kerb, heading for home. 'Just in time.'

Home in minutes, Libby slotted the safety chain firmly in place on the front door while Mandy took her mother's arm and settled her in the kitchen, still trembling. 'Did he hit you?' A cut on Elaine's forehead oozed blood.

She flinched. 'No. I – I banged it—'

'Ran into a door, did you? I don't think so.' Libby dipped cotton wool in warm water laced with Dettol and dabbed at the cut. 'It's not deep. I shouldn't think you need stitches, but you do have to ring the police.'

Elaine pushed Libby's hand away. 'No. Bert's had too much to drink, that's all it is. It'll be fine when he sobers up.'

'Mum.' Tears started in Mandy's eyes. 'It won't be fine. It's all happened before. He'll get drunk tomorrow and do it again, you know he will. Please ring the police.'

Elaine shook her head. 'I know what's best, Mandy. Just let him be. He'll cool off.'

A heavy blow shook the front door. Libby leapt to her feet.

'If Bert's cooled off, then who's that?' Another crash echoed round the house, then a third. A male voice bellowed, but Libby couldn't make out the words. The three women were on their feet, searching for something – anything – they could use to defend themselves.

Mandy grabbed Libby's arm. 'He's come after us. What are we going to do?'

'We're going to tell him to go home.' Libby's stomach lurched. Bert was well-built and strong. The bad back that kept him on sick pay was pure fiction. He could stop hammering on her door, though. How dare he? 'Stay here, you two.'

Libby straightened her shoulders, strode to the front door and pulled it open a few inches, the chain keeping it safe. Bert thrust his head into the gap. Libby could make out every mark on the man's red face: black, open pores on a bulbous nose, blobs of sweat above a mean top lip and deep lines on an angry brow.

Spit flew from the thin mouth. 'You little...'

'Don't you dare speak to me like that, Mr Parsons. There are three of us here, and we're phoning the police at this very moment.'

Mandy was close behind, holding a phone to one ear. 'Yeah, Dad. Go home and sober up.'

Bert Parsons swore and kicked the door. The chain rattled. Libby took a pace back, bile in her throat. She was vaguely aware of clattering behind her back, as Bert kicked again. Helpless, Libby watched as the screws holding the chain on the door sprang out, clinking as they hit the floor.

21

CHICKEN AND CHIPS

The third kick burst the door open. Bert shoved Libby in the chest. She over balanced, clutching the wall for support. Bert was in the house.

'Get out here, wife,' he roared.

A terrifying growl echoed round the hall.

Libby watched, mesmerised, as mouth open, teeth bared, Bear leapt at the intruder. Bert stumbled back. The dog growled again, and reared up, his enormous paws on Bert's shoulders. Bert tried to turn, slipped, and fell. Bear dropped to all fours, teeth bared, panting and slavering.

Saliva dripped on Bert's face. He struggled to rise, one arm fending off the dog. 'Get that animal away from me.' Bear planted both forepaws firmly on Bert and howled.

'Well done, Bear.' Suddenly, Max was in the hallway, hands on hips. He grinned at Libby and her stomach leaped. 'But it looks as though I've arrived too late for the excitement.'

Heart still pounding, Libby hauled the dog off Bert, and scratched Bear's ears. 'Good dog.' She slipped her fingers through the dog's collar. 'Mandy, take Bear into the sitting room.'

Elaine leaned on the doorway to the sitting room, watching in silence as Bert scrambled up, deflated and blustering. 'That dog's a menace. He needs putting down.' He shot a venomous look at Elaine. 'And you just wait 'til I get you home.'

'I won't be coming home, Albert Parsons. Not tonight, and not ever again.'

Max gripped Bert's jacket and turned the man to face him. He grabbed both lapels and tugged, forcing Bert on to his toes. Their noses almost touched. 'You'd better leave, Parsons, or you'll be the one that gets hurt.'

Bert looked from Max to Libby. 'So that's what you're up to, Max Ramshore.' His words were slurred. 'Got a new woman in town. Well, you're welcome to the ugly cow.' He shook off Max's grip and lurched down the path, stumbling and muttering.

Libby held out her hand, struggling to stop it trembling. 'Your timing is excellent, Max. Come on in and join the party.'

She stretched the meal to four, adding extra salad leaves, cutting chicken breasts in half, slicing chunks from a loaf of Frank's finest rustic bread, and opening another bottle of wine.

They ate in the kitchen. Bear settled down on the sofa in Libby's sitting room, a gentle giant once more. She hadn't the heart to move him. 'Just this once,' she said, 'Since you're a hero.'

The cat had disappeared, keeping away from the disturbance. Elaine, shaking with relief, refused to go to Accident and Emergency or call the police, but swallowed aspirin and let Mandy lead her upstairs to make up a bed.

'I'll go to my sister's in Bristol, on Monday. Bert won't come back tomorrow, not while the dog's here. And not if it means losing drinking time.'

Libby stacked plates in the dishwasher, while Mandy and her mother talked upstairs.

'Now, Max, why are you back so soon, and what did you find out?'

He insisted on making coffee, talking loudly over the grinder and frothing milk with enthusiasm. 'Well, I heard about poor old Mrs Thomson. It looks like all the action's over here after all. What is it?'

Libby was laughing. 'Mrs Thomson told me your name's really Maxwell.'

'Anyway,' he glared, 'I was worried about you. I wasn't sure how you and Bear would get on, after that business with your car. I can see I needn't have worried.'

They moved to the sitting room, where he stretched out in an armchair. 'That was a wonderful meal, by the way: better than a restaurant. I'm bushed. Jetlag, mostly. Wake me if I fall asleep.'

Fuzzy appeared from under the settee, stretched and sauntered over to sit on Max's knee.

Libby said, 'The car's been fixed and Bear's looked after me. He's even made friends with Fuzzy. I'll tell you about Guy Miles and James Sutcliffe in a minute, but first, what did you find out in America?'

'I didn't take to our friend Mickey, that's for sure. Too rich for his own good, that one, with a trophy wife, a mansion in Beverley Hills and a great opinion of himself.'

'Did you see his house?'

Max laughed. 'No, he graciously offered me half an hour of his time in a hotel. But I'd hired a car, so I did a little snooping around the area. You know, see how the other half live?'

'And?'

'I never would have thought I'd say it, but the heat was too much for me. It's good to get back to some Somerset weather.'

Libby shivered. 'Gales and rain, you mean. I suppose, at least we don't need air conditioning. Anyway, was Mickey what we expected?'

'Exactly so. I met his latest wife, by the way. Maybe you've seen her? She's starring in that sci-fi blockbuster that came out last month, and she was giving interviews at the same hotel. Mickey whisked me in and out of the room. I think he was trying to impress me.'

'Hm. He was rattled?'

'Hard to tell. Trouble is, he's got a great alibi. He spent most of Monday night at a televised award ceremony. Even with the time difference, he couldn't have attacked Susie and got back to the States in time. In any case, he hasn't really got any reason to want her dead, what with the sparkly new wife and all.'

Libby sat in silence, thinking. 'Doesn't her money go to her ex-husband if she doesn't have a will?

Max shook his head. 'Afraid not. I checked with an online solicitor, and even if she'd left money to her husband in a will, and hadn't cancelled it, he wouldn't get it when she died. The law treats the estate as though her husband was already dead. That cancels out any financial motive for our friend, Mickey.'

'Hm. So, who would be entitled to her money?'

'It depends on whether she had children, or parents, or brothers and sisters, or maybe aunts and uncles.'

'Wow. That's complicated, and it gives any of those people a motive for murder. Oh!'

'What is it?'

'I didn't tell you the police think we're right – she could have been murdered.'

Max yawned. 'That's good. We can let them chase down Susie's relatives.'

'So, that's it? We leave it to them?'

'Not quite. What about Mrs Thomson?'

Libby gasped. 'You're right. How could I have forgotten? They insist she fell down the stairs, for no good reason.'

'But you think her death's connected to Susie's?

'Of course it is. Mrs Thomson loved Susie. She showed me photos – you were in them, by the way.'

'I was? Hope that doesn't make me a suspect.'

'It seems we need to think again. I'm sure Mrs Thomson was killed because she knew something.'

Max removed Fuzzy from his knee, stretched, and crossed the room to poke at the logs on the fire, prodding until flames shot up the chimney. 'There are plenty of reasons people kill each other. Money, of course, but then there's jealousy, and revenge, and a sudden burst of uncontrollable anger – and that's even before we get to sheer craziness.' He looked up at Libby, and his voice was gentle. 'I don't want to worry you, but Mrs Thomson died after talking to you. That might mean—'

'That I'm in danger too?' Shocked, Libby sat upright, rigid. Suddenly, the investigation had taken a terrifying turn.

Max was yawning again. Libby said, 'You need to sleep. Go home. We'll be fine here.'

Max frowned. 'I can't leave you like this, but you're right, I'm bushed. Maybe I could sleep on the sofa...'

'No, you need a proper night's sleep.' She had an idea. 'Why don't I keep Bear?'

A smile transformed Max's worried face. 'That is a brilliant idea. He's already proved his worth as a guard dog. You'll be safe with him – safe from angry husbands and,' another enormous yawn overtook him, 'and whoever killed Susie. Let's have a drink tomorrow and talk further.'

As if on cue, Bear awoke, shook his head, and walked over to Libby, settling down at her feet.

She stroked his head with one hand, grabbing her phone

from the coffee table with the other. 'I'm calling a taxi. You can't possibly drive..'

As she locked the front door, Libby suddenly felt lonely, despite the presence of Mandy and Elaine upstairs. She whispered to Bear. 'Don't tell anyone, but I'm sorry he's gone.'

22

Mandy and Elaine slept in on Sunday morning. Libby enjoyed a quiet breakfast with Bear and Fuzzy. Last night's fears had disappeared and her usual good humour prevailed. She'd see Max again today and Bear would look after her. Her stomach performed an odd little flip. Exham had suddenly become a much more interesting place.

He'd phoned to suggest they meet in the Lighthouse Inn for Sunday lunchtime drinks, and something to eat. The venue seemed appropriate. Determined not to make too much effort, Libby wore a minimum of make-up: just mascara and lipstick, with the slightest blush of pink on her cheeks. Well, she excused herself, no need to go around looking tired. She pulled on jeans and a raspberry coloured sweater, brushed her hair until it shone, shrugged on a light grey jacket, loaded Bear into the Citroen – a considerable squash – and drove to the Lighthouse Inn.

Pre-dinner drinkers crowded the bar. Libby recognised some of them. Samantha Watson was in one corner, head bent close to Chief Inspector Arnold. She waved a limp hand in the air without meeting Libby's eyes.

'We must have lunch some time, Libby.'

Bear turned his back on the solicitor. Libby murmured, 'Good dog,'

Max leaned on the bar, an air force blue sweater picking up the colour of his eyes. Libby slid onto a stool. 'You look as though you slept well.'

'I'm still a touch jet-lagged, to be honest. I need a beer.'

She waited until they'd ordered. With an orange juice and lemonade in her hands, she asked, 'Why did you want to meet here?'

'I thought we should talk to a few of Susie's old friends. See who you might recognise from Mrs Thomson's photos.'

He hadn't asked her out to enjoy her sparkling wit, then. Libby asked the barman for a bowl of water for Bear, and the animal was soon surrounded by a circle of admirers.

Libby slipped the Christmas photo onto the bar. 'Mrs Thomson told me some of the names. The full names, of course. No nicknames. I wonder if Bert still answers to Albert?' She pointed to one of the boys in the picture, 'Who's that, with black hair?'

'That's Chief Inspector Arnold.'

Libby snorted. 'He's changed a bit. I suppose the beard makes a difference, and the thinning hair. I suppose everyone's changed since this was taken all those years ago, but I can recognise you. You're just the same.'

'Apart from the wrinkles.'

'I guess Bert won't be coming in today?'

'Don't bet on it. He'll be looking for sympathy. He thinks he's untouchable. There he is, with Alan and Ned.' The garage owner waved. Ned winked. Bert kept his eyes on his shoes.

Samantha, elegant in tight white jeans and a navy cashmere sweater, looking years younger than her age, with not a trace of grey showing through expensive highlights, left the inspector and shimmied over to kiss Max on both cheeks.

'Libby and I know each other.' Her eyes picked out every detail of Libby's appearance, before she turned her attention back to Max, eyelashes aflutter. 'We're in the history society together.'

Max grinned. 'History society. Really?'

'One has to find something to do here.' Samantha heaved a heavy sigh. 'It's not Bath, you know.' Her voice held a bleak note and a little of Libby's antagonism drained away. Samantha had no children. Libby's two had left home, but they phoned regularly. Lately, she even seemed to have found a surrogate child in Mandy, but Samantha, with her lovely face and figure and lucrative career, was sad, bored and lonely. Ned joined them at the bar, but his wife's lip curled in contempt.

One of the drinkers Libby had never seen before slid his pint mug along the bar. 'Is there a date for Susie's funeral, yet?' Another of Max's old friends, Libby supposed.

Max shrugged. 'Not until the police release her body.'

'Your lad, Joe, was round at our place,' the man went on. 'Asking whether we'd seen her lately.'

Samantha tossed her head. 'She pretty well walked away from us all when she was famous.'

'She was back recently.' Libby spoke without thinking. Max glared, sending her a silent message. Maybe she'd stolen his thunder. Samantha blinked, but her forehead stayed smooth. With a flash of inspiration, Libby realised why she looked so young. *Botox*. She stifled a laugh.

Max said, 'Libby, this is Ollie. We were—'

'Don't tell me. You were at school together.'

Ollie chuckled. 'You say Susie was back here? When? Did anyone see her?'

'She went to visit a member of the band. James Sutcliffe's a farmer now, making cheese, out in the sticks beyond Bristol. Susie came back to visit his wife before she died.'

Ollie whistled. 'Phew, wish we'd known. Could have had a reunion.'

Samantha laid a manicured hand on his arm. 'I don't think Susie would want to be seen with us these days, Ollie.'

Libby felt an absurd need to defend Susie. 'She kept in touch with Mrs Thomson over the years, you know, sending photos.'

Samantha's tinkling laugh jarred on Libby's ears. 'I don't know why Susie would bother with that nosy old woman. Such a busybody.'

Max's eyes flashed steel. 'Haven't you heard?'

'Heard what? I've been away the past few days. I only got back from London yesterday.' Samantha edged closer to Max, her elbow almost touching his.

He took a step away. 'Mrs Thomson's dead. She fell down the stairs.'

'Oh.' Samantha recoiled. 'Well, how would I know that? Anyway, it's true, she was a busybody, standing at that window of hers, spying on us all. She used to tell tales to my parents.' She looked round the circle of faces registering their distaste, and her voice changed to show sympathy. 'It's very sad, all the same.'

Libby said. 'Anyway, she seems to be the only one in Exham that Susie told about her—' She broke off as Max repeated the glaring routine. She coughed. 'About her visit.'

Max took her arm. 'If we're going to do that walk, Libby, we'd better get going. Joe will let us know as soon as there's a date for the funeral; either of the funerals.'

Ollie raised a refilled pint glass. 'We should all chip in, give Susie a proper send-off.'

23

THE KNOLL

Libby's back tingled as they walked away. She could swear Samantha's eyes never left her. She hissed, 'What was that all about, Max?'

He grinned. 'I wanted to see some reactions.'

'Not about Susie's daughter, though. That was what you stopped me saying, wasn't it?'

'I thought we should keep that under wraps for a while.'

She waited, but he seemed in no hurry to explain. 'OK, Max. What aren't you telling me?'

'Let's get out of here first.'

Ten minutes later, they arrived at the foot of the Knoll. Max let Bear out of the car. He jumped up, panting at the prospect of a walk. Libby wasn't so sure. The hill was steep.

'You said we were having lunch.'

'We'll do a round trip and finish up back at the pub, when everyone's left. We don't want half the town eavesdropping.'

She shrugged and set off. 'Then why did we come to a pub where you knew we'd find all your school friends?'

'Told you: for reactions. Like Samantha's. What did she have against Mrs Thomson?'

'Or against Susie?' Libby shot a glance his way. 'Max, why didn't you let me tell them about Annie Rose?' The hill grew steeper. Max's legs were long and Libby found it hard to match his stride.

'Can't we slow down a bit?' she puffed.

'What? Oh, all right.' He slowed the pace a tiny fraction.

'You're blushing, Max. Come on, spill the beans. I thought we were supposed to be working together.' She was tired of wondering about Max's history. A hint here, a tiny piece of information there: he was so secretive. 'What happened with you and Susie when you were growing up together?'

'Susie and I were good friends, back in the day. Before she left school. I suppose you'd call us childhood sweethearts.'

'And Samantha was jealous.'

He stopped, looking out over lush green fields, the motorway purring faintly in the distance, and chuckled. 'A bit, maybe. Susie and I were together for over a year. She was a dear, sweet girl. At first, anyway. She was always musical, unlike me, and loved to sing. Guy asked her to join the band. That was fine, at first, but then the band took off and things changed. Susie started to drink too much – even for a teenager. She started smoking pot. Everyone was doing it in those days. Well, not everyone. I wasn't one of the cool kids.'

Libby laughed. 'Me, neither.'

Their eyes met. 'I wish I'd known you then,' Max said.

Libby swallowed.

Max set off again, slowly. 'Sorry, where was I?' He coughed. 'When Susie drank, she was wild. She didn't seem to know when to stop.'

'I suppose it's easy to get carried away if you're in a successful band.' Libby's breathlessness had nothing to do with the incline.

Max walked faster. 'Guy didn't go to our school. He was at a public school in Bristol: his father was a wealthy man. Guy kept Susie supplied with pot, I'm afraid. She started to spend more time with him than with me. I suppose I could see the writing on the wall.'

Max's face took on a faraway look, as though he was reliving the past: a past when he was in love with Susie. He breathed hard. 'Susie had a Saturday job in the newsagents. One afternoon, I went in to get cigarettes.'

He glanced sideways, caught Libby's eye, and grimaced. 'Everyone smoked, back then. The owner went into the back room. When Susie put my money in the till, she lifted a handful of cash. It wasn't much, but it gave me a jolt. We had a row, and I accused her of being a drunk and a thief. She laughed at me.'

Max bent over, picked up a handful of stones and tossed them into a hollow. 'She said: "You go around with your eyes shut, Max. If you only knew…" I had no idea what she was talking about. I suppose I was a bit dim in those days. I wouldn't let it go. I got mad, accused her of preferring Guy to me, of sleeping with him. She just roared with laughter and I stormed off. Neither of us apologised and we broke up. That's it, really. An everyday story of teenagers.'

Libby stopped walking. 'But you must have known she wasn't sleeping with Guy.'

'What? Of course, she was. She didn't deny it.'

'Max, he's gay. He's living with a man called Alvin. They're a couple.'

'You're kidding.' He scratched his head. 'Guy? Who'd have thought it? Are you sure?'

She nodded. He gave a crack of laughter. 'More fool me. Well,

Susie and I didn't get back together.' He stopped, frowning, as though thinking hard. He murmured, 'Not Guy? Then who?' He shrugged. 'Well, the band played at Glastonbury, Mickey came along, whisked her off to the States and married her.'

Libby's head was spinning. 'Can we sit down for a bit?'

They were almost at the top of the knoll, and the wind whipped at their clothes. Bear galloped up and down, full of energy, while they perched on stones. Libby's heart rate slowed to something more normal as she gazed out across the patchwork of fields. Rooks swooped, cawing, high above. The wind blew Max's hair over his eyes and he shoved it back with an impatient hand.

Of course, Max still had a soft spot for Susie, his first love. It was touching, really. Those teenage years, when life was so intense. That must have been around the time Libby met Trevor. She shook the thought away and spoke lightly. 'Well, that's quite a story. I guess we all have stuff in our past. Anyway, did you see Susie again after she left the country?'

'No. I was too proud. I wasn't going to chase after her. I wish I had. Not to get back together again, we'd grown too far apart, but to keep an eye on her. She could have used some real friends, I think.'

'My mother used to say, "If wishes were horses then beggars would ride". Come on, I'll race you to the top.'

Max overtook Libby easily. She stood and watched as he climbed on, towards the summit. What were those motives he'd mentioned? Money, jealousy, revenge. Max could have nursed his anger at Susie all these years and seized the opportunity for revenge when she came back.

She clenched her fists. Surely not Max? It couldn't be...

He turned to wait for her, and she remembered he'd been abroad when Mrs Thomson was killed. Relief left her legs shaky. She closed her eyes for a moment. She'd been in danger of letting imagination run away with her. She put on a spurt of speed to catch up.

Bear reached the summit first. He rolled in a patch of hazy sunshine. Max reached back to pull Libby, panting, up the last few yards. She groaned. 'I need to get into shape.'

'You look good enough to me.' She blinked, surprised, and a little warm glow ignited inside.

To cover her confusion, she told Max about her visits to Guy and James yesterday. 'They both cared for her and James kept in contact. He showed me a letter she wrote, just before the divorce. He said losing Annie Rose broke her heart.'

'Losing a child. Nothing could be worse,' Max murmured.

They sat quietly. Libby thought she'd rarely been happier than today, with Bear and Max.

'What do you do for a living, Max? You said you had business in America.'

'Finance stuff. I consult, which sounds much grander than it is. I work for organisations that need my rather dull ability to trace financial transactions.'

'Oh.'

'Exactly. Not exciting at all, but I get to travel from time to time, although most of the work can be done online.' He plucked a handful of grass and threw it into the wind. 'Which is a good thing, at my age. Jetlag's a killer.'

Libby watched as the grass blew away.

Max said. 'I've been thinking about Mickey again.'

The autumn sun warmed Libby's face as she leaned her back against the jutting rock. 'Sorry, what did you say?'

'Mickey. I'd crossed him off our list of suspects, but I'm still not sure. He was shifty when I met him. We may not know of a motive for him, but that doesn't mean one doesn't exist, and a man with his wealth can have a long reach. He may not need money, but what about jealousy, or revenge?'

He sat up, leaning on his elbows, his eyes on Libby. 'You should take care. I'll leave Bear with you for a while. Keep your eyes open and don't go out alone, especially at night. Meanwhile,' he jumped up, brushed mud from his trousers and pulled Libby to her feet. 'Let's have that lunch.'

24

DIARY

A weak autumn sun shone above Exham the next morning. A niggle of dread had haunted Libby after the conversation with Max, but it evaporated with the night. Of course, she was in no danger. They'd been over-dramatising.

She hummed as she showered and dressed, before driving Mandy and Elaine to Exham on Sea station for the first leg of their journey to Bristol. They waved as they crossed the railway bridge to the east-bound platform. Mandy planned to stay, settling her mother in with her aunt before returning in a day or so. 'I'll try to get Mum to talk to the police.' She had a determined glint in her eye.

Libby planned to take Bear back to Max. She'd kept him here for one last night, but there was no space in her tiny house for such an enormous animal. She could look after herself, and Bear needed to run free in Max's grounds.

'Make the most of it,' she told Fuzzy as she gathered up the day's post from the mat. 'We're both going to miss that dog.'

She flipped through the handful of letters: a catalogue, two flyers and something official from Trevor's solicitor, acting as his executor. More on the slow progress of probate, presumably. It seemed to take forever, even though he'd left everything to Libby.

She ripped the letter open.

Dear Mrs Forest…

She sank on to the bottom stair, deaf to the racket Fuzzy and Bear made as they chased one another round the house. The letter shook in her hand.

Nausea gripped her stomach as she read the words again, hoping she'd misunderstood.

We regret to inform you…

The solicitor used careful, legal language, but the meaning was clear. There was no money. Trevor had spent every penny, and more. He'd had accounts in places Libby had never dreamed about, all with overdrafts and loans. The solicitor had tracked them down, paid back as many as possible and set out the account for Libby to see.

Trevor's debts far exceeded the total of the estate. Libby was broke. What's more, she owed several thousand pounds to Trevor's creditors. Shakily, she heaved her body up. A headache gripped her temples. She threw the letter on the kitchen counter, mechanically spooned instant coffee into a mug, searched for aspirin and wondered what in the world she was going to do.

It was already late. She had to go to work. She couldn't afford to lose the job: in fact, she'd have to ask Frank for more hours.

She brushed her hair and found a coat. Recovering from its temporary paralysis, her mind buzzed. The business course would have to wait. Thank heaven she'd sold the London house. It had been in both names. Trevor had slipped up there. This house had been much cheaper, so Libby had some funds in her bank account, but not many. Would they be enough? Not for a new bathroom.

Profits from 'Baking on the Beach' were tiny. They wouldn't last long. She'd have to sign Mr Fisher's contract.

Susie's death had taken over Libby's life this past week. She'd become obsessed with Susie, Mrs Thomson and Max. She needed to sort out her life, fast.

The morning at the bakery passed in a fog. Business had returned to normal; the excitement over Susie's death little more than a nine day wonder. Libby could hardly talk for the knot in her stomach. She had no clear idea, afterwards, who she'd spoken to or what she'd said. She'd ask Frank about extra work tomorrow. She'd burst into tears if she tried to broach the subject today.

She left as soon as her shift ended and drove home, where Bear and Fuzzy snored, curled together in a bundle of fur, in Bear's apple crate. Libby pulled out the contract, signed it, stuffed it in an envelope, sealing the flap in place so she couldn't change her mind.

Committed to the new book, she started the computer, dragged a file full of her original recipes from a shelf and stared at a blank page, watching the cursor flicker, telling her brain to concentrate on recipes.

After two hours, depression set in. How could she concentrate on rosewater and lemon sponge cake with the horror of her financial position hanging over her head. She couldn't bear to sell Hope Cottage, the home she'd loved since the moment she saw it, despite its horrendous bathroom. The house's rickety charms had wrapped themselves around her heart.

Her shoulders ached and a lump of cement seemed to have settled in her stomach. She should eat, for she'd had no lunch, but she needed to work. Her stomach rumbled. Maybe sucking a mint might help stave off the hunger pangs. She pulled out the drawer where she kept a supply of blindingly strong mints in a tiny green tin.

Mrs Thomson's papers lay where she'd dropped them, on top of the tin. Not now. Libby slammed the drawer shut. She had no time to think about Mrs Thomson. She had a living to earn. She'd spent far too long trekking through the countryside and discovered precious little for her pains. She was no nearer finding the killer of Susie than the day she found the body.

The police, or Max, or someone else – anyone – could find out what happened to Susie without her help.

She leaned both elbows on the desk. The cursor still winked, relentlessly, but she ignored it. Guilt had brought on a cold sweat. She'd visited Mrs Thomson, talked about Susie, and the old lady had died. Was that a coincidence, or was the death connected to Libby's visit?

Libby groaned. She had to know. She ran her hands over Mrs Thomson's possessions. They looked trivial; the usual random collection of documents found in any house. The police, busy with Susie's death, believing the old lady fell down the stairs by accident, would be likely to stuff them in a file and forget them.

That wouldn't do. Someone pushed Mrs Thomson downstairs and thought they'd got away with it. Libby meant to prove they were wrong. She would hand the documents over to the police, like a responsible citizen – but first, she'd read every word. She owed that to Mrs Thomson.

She cleared a space on the desk, lifted the heap of papers and books from the drawer, and laid everything in neat piles; the photograph album on the right, with a couple of notebooks on top. Holiday brochures for self-catering apartments in Cornwall, advertisements for pain relief gels to relieve rheumatism, and an invitation for Mrs Thomson to attend the hearing clinic at the local War Memorial hospital on the left.

She flipped through that pile first, found nothing remotely sinister, and dumped the pile back in the drawer.

Now, she could concentrate on the album and the two notebooks.

She lifted the first, a small blue book, each page dated like a diary. Lines of small, crabbed handwriting covered most pages.

Libby chose a page at random.

Monday 15 March

2.30 p.m. Judy Roach took her three boys down to the beach. They walked all the way to the lighthouse. Philip had a new red bucket and made sandcastles, but his older brothers kicked them down.
7 p.m. Five girls ran wild on the beach this evening, trying to light a bonfire but the driftwood was too wet. Too young to be out alone – never mind playing with matches. Do their parents know what they're up to? Note: mention it in the office at St Mary's school.

So far, so dull. An everyday story of a sleepy seaside town before the summer visitors arrive, written by a lonely old lady, a busybody, watching the children she cared about and trying to keep them safe.

A flash of inspiration set Libby's pulse racing. She turned to the back of the book, fingers fumbling. What if Mrs Thomson saw what happened on the day Susie died? Her house was ideally situated, with that view across the expanse of sand. Libby herself had seen the lighthouse while Mrs Thomson had been in the kitchen. Perhaps Mrs Thomson had noticed something important and recorded it here, in the diary.

Libby checked the dates on the final pages. The notes stopped the day before Susie's death. Disappointment kicked in. She read the last few pages, but as far as she could see, there was not a single clue to be found in the book.

She tossed the diary on the desk in disgust and trailed down to make a sandwich. Fuzzy appeared in front of her from nowhere, running around her legs as she negotiated the uneven stairs. 'Be careful, Fuzzy. I don't want to be the next to fall downstairs.

She picked up the cat and buried her fingers in soft fur. 'You're friendly, today. Bear's having a good effect on you. By the way, if you've been wondering what's going on, you're not the only one.' Bear snored in the apple crate downstairs, twitching, dreaming of bones or chasing rabbits. With a sudden wail, Fuzzy leaped from Libby's arms. She ran back up the stairs to the study, Libby close behind, wondering what had got into the cat.

Fuzzy leapt on the desk. 'Watch out.' Libby grabbed the cat's tail as papers slithered across the surface on to the floor. Fuzzy settled on the shambles, rolled on her back and purred. 'Oh, they smell of Bear, do they? Is that what you're telling me? Well, I'll be finished with them soon. There aren't any clues there, after all.'

Libby retrieved single sheets of paper from the floor and tapped them into a neat pile. Two smaller pages had slid away. She gathered them up, noticing the ragged edges where they had been ripped from a spiral notepad, similar to one a journalist might use – like the second notebook she'd found with the diary.

The pages in that notepad were blank, but the two loose pages bore Mrs Thomson's unmistakable scribbled writing, complete with dates.

She set the notebook to one side and examined the loose

pages. Dated 6th and 7th June, each page bore random letters and numbers.

Libby thought for a moment, then picked up the blue diary and shuffled through until she found the entries for June, comparing them with the single letters.

10 p g

Mrs Thomson had scribbled in her notebook. From the diary, Libby discovered the playgroup had been on the beach at ten in the morning.

If only she had entries for the day Susie died.

She laid the books and papers back on the desk, the notebook open at the blank page. The light from the computer monitor reflected back from the paper. Libby squinted. She could see indentations on the notebook page – the kind left by pressure from a pen. That meant there must be another sheet of paper somewhere – the page where Mrs Thomson had scrawled her note.

She searched through the pile of papers, hope flickering only to die a moment later. There was no sign of the missing top sheet. Frustrated, Libby grabbed the indented page and held it up to the light. An S and a couple of numbers. 14? She peered more closely. Yes, and those marks were W and E. Try as she might, though, Libby failed to make out any full words.

The doorbell rang. Annoyed at the interruption, convinced she'd made an important discovery, she weighed down the loose pages with the tin of mints and scooped up the cat.

25

RUBBISH

Max, a worried frown on his face, stood on the doorstep.

'I came to say you should hang on to Bear a little longer, until this business is over. He'll keep you safe.'

Libby, not listening, grabbed Max's arm and tugged him inside the house.

'Never mind that, now. Follow me.' She led him upstairs, ignoring his protests. 'Look. Can you see?'

She thrust the blue notebook under Max's nose. He squinted. 'Looks like a diary. Is it yours? Are you sure you want me to see it?'

This was no time for jokes. 'These are Mrs Thomson's notes. She watched the beach from the window, writing about everything she saw in the spiral notebook, in a sort of shorthand. Then she transcribed it in full into her diary and made notes to herself. She worried about the children in the area.'

She opened the spiral notebook, laid it on her desk, then rustled through the blue diary to find the right page. 'You see the dates. They cover most of September...' She pointed to each book.

Understanding lit Max's eyes as he read the short entries in the notebook. 'These are from the week before Susie died.' He flipped to the end. 'The last day's missing. What a shame she didn't make any notes on the day Susie died.'

'I thought that, but I was wrong. She did make notes, but they've gone.'

Libby took a breath, desperate to make Max understand. 'At first, I thought she hadn't been watching the beach that day, but then I saw these marks on the next page of the notebook. You see, the page for 14th September has gone – it's been torn out.'

'How do you know?'

'You can make out some of the letters on the blank page, where she pressed down hard.' She stabbed at the blank page. 'I think maybe the – the killer took the page for that day when he killed her?'

Max's eyes narrowed. 'We have to know what she wrote. The police have specialist equipment so they can read it. We'll take all this to Joe.' He waved a hand at the papers.

It was an anti-climax. Libby murmured, disappointed. 'Can't we try to understand it ourselves?'

Max laughed. 'You're not a fan of the police, I take it. Well, since they're convinced her death was an accident, I don't suppose they'll be in any hurry to look at her notes. How did you get these, by the way?'

Libby's face burned. 'I suppose I stole them from Mrs Thomson's house.'

'Did you, indeed?' Max shook his head. 'Joe will have something to say about that.' He grinned at Libby, looking ten years younger, as excited as she. 'Well, before we confess to my son, who'll make a song and dance about it, let's see what we can read.'

Taking a lead pencil from the pot on Libby's desk, he rubbed it lightly over the surface of the paper, leaving the indentations visible.

'You can't see all the letters, but there should be enough to tell us if it's useful.'

Libby, reaching over his shoulder, grabbed a sheet of copy paper and wrote:

4 J boys castles.
5 rain.
5.15 T walking L
6 Windy, wet. B rubbish.
7 Tide.

They stood side by side, considering the letters.

Libby said, 'I think that's right. I can guess at some of the words, but it still doesn't make much sense.'

Max grinned. 'It's Mrs Thomson's own shorthand. All we have to do is crack the code. How are you with crosswords?' He reached over the table. 'Maybe the diary will help.'

He opened the blue notebook and, heads together, they pored over the pages from March, comparing them with the shorthand.

Max said, 'I see. She notes the time of day, who came to the beach, and what happened. It's not too complicated.'

They turned to the page of indentations from 14th September.

Libby stabbed at the first entry. 'The J is Judy Roach, like in the earlier entry. She walks on the beach with her three boys and they build sandcastles.'

'At five o'clock, it rained,' Max murmured.

Libby said, 'At a quarter past five, T was walking L – a dog, I suppose. Do we know who that might be?'

'We should be able to find out easily enough. It's probably a regular.'

Libby remembered. 'There's a lady with a dachshund called Lily – the dog, not the lady. I don't know her name, but I've met her on the beach when I've been walking Shipley.'

Max frowned. 'Shipley?'

'He's the dog I walk sometimes for Marina. It's not important.'

'Right. Ever thought of getting your own dog?' Max turned back to the code. 'At 6 o'clock it was windy and wet. Wasn't it getting dark? How could she see?'

He pulled out his phone. 'I've got an app for sunrise and sunset.' Libby laughed. 'Robert – my son – has dozens of apps.'

'Sounds like my kind of chap. Does he look like you?'

'Not in the slightest. He's my husband's child. Ali, my daughter, takes after me.'

'Lucky girl.'

'Anyway,' Libby returned to business, secretly delighted. 'What does your app tell us?'

'Sunset was at 7.35 that evening. So, at six, it would still be light enough to see anything interesting on the beach.'

'And the lighthouse flashes regularly. That would help.'

'Good point.' Max nodded. 'This B must be another name, someone around in the dusk. It could be a teenager, or an adult. I can't imagine mothers were bringing their children out at that time in the wind and rain. So, what was B doing, and what does *rubbish* mean?' Libby shook her head.

Max waved the problem away. 'Never mind. We can come back to that. There's just one entry left. At 7 o'clock, she wrote *tide.* I guess she means high tide. It came right in, that night, to the dunes.' He straightened up, rubbing his back. 'We have a couple of mysteries left. On the night of Susie's death, Mrs Thomson saw B just as the tide was coming in. B must be a person. I wonder what B was doing. Mrs Thomson just wrote *rubbish.*'

Libby looked through the notebook, but there was no other

entry like that. B must be an initial, like J and T. But why *rubbish?* After an hour, they'd pored over every word in the blue book. There were lots of names beginning with B, but there was no way to know who'd been on the beach on the day Susie died, or why.

Max sucked a mint. 'It could be someone who's never appeared in the book before. That would mean they don't often come to the beach. It rules out dog walkers.'

Libby said, 'I think this is important. Someone tore the page from Mrs Thomson's notebook. She wouldn't have taken it out until she'd transcribed it into her diary. She was fanatical. All the other pages match, except this one. It makes me think...'

Max said, 'Me too. I'm going to take an educated guess – I think she saw someone dumping what she thought was rubbish, and she recognised him – or her.'

He perched on the edge of Libby's desk. 'Maybe I'm jumping to conclusions, but why would anyone dump rubbish under the lighthouse.'

Libby shivered. 'What if it wasn't rubbish, but something else in a bag.'

'You mean...'

'Could it have been – been a body in the bag?'

'Rubbish, or a body. I wonder which?'

'No one would go to the trouble of dumping a bag of rubbish on the beach – it would be far too much effort.'

Max nodded along. 'Let's assume for a moment it was Susie's body. It would be heavy. Susie was small, but she'd be a dead weight. I think it must have been a man. Someone Mrs Thomson knew as B.'

Libby shivered. 'B could have looked up and seen her at the window. He knew she'd seen him, and, from that moment, Mrs Thomson was in danger.'

Max agreed. 'She knew the murderer. She thought he was

dumping rubbish – bad behaviour, illegal, and enough for her to make a note of it. She didn't realise he was dangerous, so she didn't tell the police or worry about it...'

'Until B called on her, a couple of days later, to check that she hadn't put two and two together.'

Libby said, 'Susie wasn't in a bag when I found her.'

'No, but the tide was high that night, and the wind blew a gale. Between them, they could easily have ripped the bag away.'

Libby remembered the missing boot. If the storm tide had enough strength to wrench a leather boot from Susie's foot, it could easily shred a thin black plastic bin liner. She bit her lip. 'So, B was getting rid of the body, knew he'd been seen, and visited Mrs Thomson to make sure.'

'She knew him, let him in, and probably gave him a good telling off for dumping litter.'

'He could ask her to fetch something from upstairs – a jacket, perhaps, saying he was cold. He'd follow her upstairs and shove her down. She was a frail old lady, left alone to die.' Libby blinked away sudden tears. 'I wonder how long she lay there.'

Max's face was grim. 'Let's hope she died instantly.'

Libby said, 'I think we should call the police.'

Detective Sergeant Joe Ramshore called at Libby's house within the hour. Libby confessed to taking Mrs Thomson's papers, and Max chimed in to relate their theory.

Joe scolded Libby for interfering with a police investigation as if she were a naughty schoolgirl, scowled at his father. Max's involvement seemed to infuriate him even more.

'You're not above the law, either of you.'

'I'm very sorry,' Libby mumbled, humbly.

Max said, 'But you wouldn't have looked through Mrs Thomson's belongings. You were so sure she died from an accidental fall.'

'Hm. Well, we won't charge you for removing evidence. At least, not yet.'

'Can you find out who B is?' Libby asked.

'We'll check on the electoral register. You see,' he lectured, 'it's the day-to-day police work that will solve this, Mrs Forest, not amateur dabbling.'

Libby kept her temper in check, fighting the urge to point out the days he'd wasted.

Once Joe and Max had left, Libby undertook a whirl of activity. She phoned Ned, the builder, to explain she couldn't afford to go ahead with the alterations to the bathroom.

'Don't you worry about it, Mrs F. I'll keep the plans we made, and you let me know as soon as you want to start.' Libby felt dreadful. That was the trouble with a small town: you knew and liked the people who worked for you.

She wrote to the solicitor, asking for suggestions as to how to sort out the mess of Trevor's debts, and sent emails to Robert ad Ali. There, they won't think I'm just an aging mother, she thought, jabbing 'send' with a triumphant finger. Then, needing a break, she went to the local history society meeting, bearing the latest version of the lemon and rosewater cake.

The group, between mouthfuls, reviewed the recent event at Mangotsfield Hall.

'It was a huge success.' Angela was the treasurer. 'We split the profits with the Hall, and we've made enough to pay for a year's worth of speakers. Not that we don't have some excellent ones of our own.'

She nodded at Beryl, an elderly lady dressed in grey, who sat in the corner fingering a stack of notes.

'Everyone loved Marina's talk.'

'I thought I'd die when Libby was down to her shift,' There was a ripple of laughter. Libby had almost forgotten those awful Victorian clothes. There were so many layers. She frowned. A thought tugged at the back of her mind but she couldn't get hold of it. It was about the costume. Or, was it? She concentrated, but she couldn't recall. Oh well, maybe it would come back to her.

She kept silent about the discoveries she'd made. She'd annoyed the police enough, for now.

Bear stayed with her, 'For protection,' Max insisted. He

popped in, every evening, and took Bear for a run. 'Is he behaving,' he asked.

'Good as gold,' Libby said. 'Fuzzy gives him a smack on the nose if he gets too excited. But he can't stay for ever – he needs room to run.'

'Only until the police make an arrest,' Max insisted. Libby didn't argue. She enjoyed the giant dog's company, and secretly liked Max to visit.

With a spurt of hard work lasting well into the small hours of every morning, Libby settled down to write the cookery book, praying for an early publication date and the chance to pay off some of Trevor's debts. Frank, thrilled with sales for her recipes, had taken her on full-time, given her a rise and a new job title: Development Consultant.

She still felt sick when she thought of the money Trevor had owed. The bathroom made her want to cry, with its bright orange tiles, a shower that dripped slow, barely warm water, and a cracked window. She'd have to live with it for at least another year. She could almost believe Trevor had planned it all out of spite. It was like a final insult from beyond the grave. Libby would work her socks off to get free of him.

At last, the coroner released Susie's body, and the funeral was arranged for the next day – Thursday afternoon. Mandy, having arrived back from a stay with her mother and aunt, insisted on making dinner, using Libby's sausage casserole recipe.

'Oh, it's so good to be back.' Mandy groaned. 'They drive me mad, those two. Always on at me for my tats, and the piercings.'

Libby kept silent about the tattoos that climbed Mandy's arms and encircled her neck. 'Mandy, you're old enough to look after yourself. Get a flat.'

Mandy blushed and cleared her throat. 'I don't suppose you'd like me to stay – be a permanent lodger, would you?'

'I'd love it, but that's not exactly standing on your own two feet, is it?' *But I could use the cash.*

'I can't afford a proper flat of my own.'

'Well, in that case. Just for a while.'

* * *

The evening before the funeral was dark and still. The storms had passed over, and another flurry from the Atlantic was not expected for a while. Libby stood at the window of her study and stretched, muscles tense from an hour at the computer. There was so little light pollution that stars filled the whole expanse of sky. Maybe she'd get a telescope, one day in the distant future when she'd cleared the debts, and learn more about them.

The street lay deserted. Only one car passed, turning into a nearby driveway, its engine dying. Libby heard the clunk of a garage door. She opened the window to smell the sea and took a deep breath. This beat London's bright lights.

A movement on the left caught her attention. Instinctively, she drew back inside the window as a figure crept, soundless, close to the wall of the house, around the corner and past the sycamore tree, finally disappearing into shadow. That was odd. Libby didn't expect a visitor. Ears straining, she listened for a knock on the door, but all was quiet. She slipped downstairs and hovered just inside the front door, watching through the tiny pane of glass, but there was no sign of a caller.

Uneasy, heart pounding, she crept past the sitting room where Mandy was watching a game show, into the kitchen. The curtains and blinds were drawn tight against the autumn night. With a clatter, Bear brushed past, almost knocking Libby off her feet as he leaped at the back door, barking, the noise battering Libby's ears. He'd heard a noise, too. Libby scrambled to the door, fumbling with the lock, and flung it open.

There was no one there. One hand on the dog, the other clenched tight, Libby stepped outside into cool, still air. She sniffed. Was that a whiff of beer? She hadn't imagined it, then. Someone had been here.

She tiptoed round the side of the house and back again. The stalker was long gone. In the distance, a car engine revved and faded. Mandy was at the back door. 'What was all that about? I heard Bear going crazy.'

Libby hesitated. Mandy needed to be on her guard. She shrugged. 'I thought someone was outside.'

'Who'd be creeping about in the dark?'

'I don't know.' She locked the door, shaking it to check it was secure, sat Mandy down and told her what they'd found in Mrs Thomson's diary. 'Maybe whoever was sneaking around knew I took it from her house.'

'It's a good thing Bear's staying.' Mandy shrugged, unfazed. 'He won't let anyone near you.'

Libby lay awake for a long time that night, chills running up and down her spine. If the stalker was the same person who'd pushed Mrs Thomson down the stairs, the mysterious B, both she and Mandy were in danger.

Her brain whirled, images chasing each other in a confused kaleidoscope of the past few days. There was Susie, slumped under the lighthouse like a sack of rubbish; Mrs Thomson, gazing out of her window at a world that passed her by; the local history group, gossiping; the 'Band of Brothers' of local men, looking to Max for guidance; James Sutcliffe and Guy each living a new life as though the wild days of the band had never happened.

In her mind's eye, Libby recalled the pictures of Susie, with

Mickey on her wedding day, and of her daughter, Annie Rose. Sleep wouldn't come, now. Libby pushed back the duvet, thrust cold feet into slippers and softly, so as not to wake Mandy, slipped along to the study. She grabbed a clean, fresh sheet of copy paper and began to write.

27

FUNERAL

The weather forecast for Susie's funeral promised a day of cold, watery sunshine. Libby, torn between an old grey trench coat and the long, formal, black wool coat she'd bought for Trevor's funeral, peered anxiously at the sky.

'I'll wear the wool coat, otherwise I might never use it again.' She winced as Mandy, appropriate for once in her customary head-to-toe black, fiddled with her latest piercing at the top of one ear. 'Doesn't that hurt?'

At the church, Max squeezed Libby's arm. 'Every shop in Exham must be shut.' The town streamed in past a phalanx of photographers. 'Even the national newspapers are here. Pity Susie isn't around to enjoy it.'

'There's Guy.' Guy brushed past the photographers, eyes straight ahead. Alvin stopped to flick a speck of dust off his jacket. James Sutcliffe was there, too, his son steering him past the press who were, in any case, far too busy interviewing Samantha Watson to notice, let alone recognise, the once famous members of Susie's band. Tossing her fringe, one elegant foot in front of the other, Samantha nailed, with ease, the self-appointed role of Susie's best friend.

After the service, a smaller band of mourners met at the crematorium to say a final goodbye to their old friend. As the coffin slid behind the curtain, Susie's voice followed them from the room, swelling through speakers, filling the building with her most famous song, 'What's In a Name'. James Sutcliffe blew his nose and a lump lodged in Libby's throat.

The local hotel, efficiently run by Marina's sister, put on a spread, the garden bathed in Indian summer sunshine. Libby juggled a plate and glass, leaning on a wall at the front, watching the other mourners.

Max took a place by her side, 'It's good to see the hotel packed with Susie's old friends.'

As he spoke, a black stretch limousine screeched to a halt outside the hotel. The uniformed chauffeur leaped out to fling open a rear door and a middle-aged, overweight man eased from the car, long grey hair caught in a ponytail. Gold earrings flashed and a medallion sparkled at the neck of his open-neck black silk shirt.

Max murmured, 'There he is: Mickey Garston himself.'

Two thick-set men, startling with shaved heads and earpieces, leapt from a second car and took up positions close behind Mickey, eyes hidden by reflective sunglasses. Mandy let out a low whistle. Mickey's transatlantic accent, loud enough to rattle glasses on the wooden tables dotted around the hotel garden, boomed over the crowd.

'Hey, I guess I missed the funeral. That's too bad. Caught up in your English traffic. You need some system around here.'

Max's mouth was close to Libby's ear. 'What do you think he wants?' as the man approached.

The newcomer stretched out an arm. 'Max, my old buddy,

good to see you again.' He grabbed Max's hand, the other arm snaking round his shoulders. 'Won't you introduce me to Susie's friends?'

Max extricated himself, unsmiling. 'I see you came after all.'

'Max, introduce me. Who's this gorgeous creature?' Samantha, white teeth flashing, poised on four inch stiletto heels. She extended one graceful arm, tinkling with bracelets, to take the flabby hand.

Light bulbs popped. Bored journalists set down half-eaten sausage rolls, flipped their note pads to clean pages and pulled out cheap pens.

A hoarse bellow splintered the air. 'What the hell are you doing here?' James Sutcliffe, fists raised, elbowed past Libby. 'Get back to the pond you crawled out of.'

Mickey's bodyguards rearranged themselves on either side of the boss. Max's single step dissected the space between James and the Americans. Jack Sutcliffe grasped his father's arm. 'Come away, Dad, it's too late for that. Leave it.'

James shook the arm away, his face purple. 'You've got a nerve, Garston, showing your face here after what you did.'

Mickey flinched. 'Come on now, no need for this. I'm just paying my respects—'

James shook his fist. 'You should be in prison for what you did.'

Max and Libby exchanged a look. What was James talking about? Did he think the fat American killed Susie?

'What I did? What...'

James bellowed, 'You killed your little girl.'

In the sudden silence,, someone dropped their drink, the glass shattering on the stone path.

Mickey swallowed. He raised his hands, palms out, bluster gone. 'No need for that, now.' He leaned forward, peering at

James. 'Is that you? James Sutcliffe? After all these years?' He let his hands fall. 'Now, come on, man. It wasn't my fault the little girl died. It was an accident. Why, I was as upset as anyone.'

James's voice shook. 'Susie trusted Annie Rose with you, just for one day. All you had to do was play with the child and keep her safe. So, what did you do?' He clenched his fists. Tears soaked the weather-beaten cheeks.

'You sat in front of the TV, drinking beer and eating fast food like a pig.' A sob sounded in his throat. 'How long was Annie Rose in the pool, dead, before you even noticed she'd gone?'

Mickey shifted, edging backwards towards the car, shooting a look at his bodyguards. 'Come on, now, James. The kid could swim. She was fine, playing with the dog I gave her as a present. I guess he jumped in the pool and she followed. It wasn't my fault,' he blustered. 'Susie had no right to leave the kid with me, anyway. She wasn't even mine.'

'Not yours? What do you mean, not yours?'

Mickey laughed through twisted lips. 'You still don't know, do you? Susie fooled us all. She sure made a monkey out of me. Yes, your precious Susie Bennett was already pregnant when we met. She tried to pass the baby off as mine. Made out the birth was premature. I was a sucker.'

Someone gasped. Guy's face creased in a frown. He broke the stunned silence. 'We never knew. She didn't say. It was that summer at Glastonbury. Susie was sick every day. Do you remember, James?'

'We thought it was the mud.' James Sutcliffe shrugged. 'It rained so hard, that year, there was mud everywhere. Couldn't get away from it. Slept in it, sat in it. It got into the food, the beer. In the end, we gave up trying to keep clean. People were ill, plenty of 'em, not just Susie. Caught things from the bacteria in the mud.'

'And we thought Susie had a bug.' Guy pushed his glasses up

his nose. 'But maybe we were wrong. Maybe she was sick because she was pregnant.'

Max joined in. 'Susie left town suddenly after Glastonbury. No one expected it.'

Guy said, 'She was excited about our big break. She couldn't wait to get over to the States. She left with him,' he gestured at Mickey, 'and we followed a few weeks later.'

Libby studied the puzzled faces of Susie's old school friends. Most registered shock and surprise – but not quite all. A bubble of excitement grew inside Libby's chest.

'You all knew Susie, you'd grown up with her, but she didn't trust anyone with her secret.' One pair of eyes slid away. Libby's pulse raced. Could she be right?

Mickey folded his arms. 'Yeah. She was expecting someone else's baby, and she kept it a secret until after she'd got me up the aisle.'

His lips twisted. 'She thought she was so clever, putting one over on me. But I'm no fool. I wouldn't have got where I am, if I couldn't work a few things out. That was no premature baby, I can tell you.' He pointed a finger at Guy. 'Soon as the kid was born, I put two and two together, and they made five. Anyway, Annie Rose looked nothing like me. She had blue eyes. Nobody in my family ever had blue eyes.'

He swaggered past the security guards. 'I did right by Susie. I was straight with her and she made a fool out of me, but even then, I didn't kick her out.'

'Course you didn't,' Guy jeered. 'You were making a fortune out of her – out of us all. She was your meal ticket. Because of Susie, you were rich enough, and powerful enough, to keep the scandal out of the press.'

Mickey called to the bodyguards. 'Come on, boys, let's get out of here. I came over to pay my respects, and all I get is abuse—'

'Who are you trying to fool, Mickey?' Max said. 'You don't care about Susie. You came over here to find out if she left you any money. Well, she didn't, but you'll go on getting what you always wanted from her — money. Her songs are already climbing the charts. For you, she's the gift that goes on giving, so clear on out of here, and don't come back. Count your dollars on the other side of the pond.'

Mickey paused, one foot in the limousine. His lip curled in a snarl. 'She owed me.'

Clouds scudded across the sun and heavy drops of rain spattered the tables. As guests ran for cover, the gossip began, eager questions fizzing in the air. Guy's voice rose above the others.

'If Mickey wasn't Annie Rose's father, then who was?'

28

Max's spoon clinked against a glass. Slowly, the hubbub died away. 'Guy, that's a very good question, and it's at the heart of the mystery of Susie's death.' He encompassed everyone with a sweep of his arm.

'Nearly everyone from the old days is here today. Susie's death was a shock for most of us. But not for one. Not for the father of Susie's baby.'

A murmur rose, almost drowning Max's words. He raised his voice.

'Susie never told anyone the child wasn't Mickey's, but she had a plan, just in case he found out. She put money away for her little girl. It was insurance, in case Mickey found out he'd been tricked into marrying Susie and left her to provide for the child. She never needed it, because Annie Rose died.'

He beckoned to Libby. 'Why don't you tell them the rest? You've worked it all out.'

Libby cleared her throat. 'The person who killed Susie and dumped her body under the lighthouse came from this town.' On Libby's left, Mandy clutched her mother's arm, white knuckles bright against Elaine's black jacket. To her right, Susie's old schoolmates clustered together, faces registering surprise, excitement and, for some, horror.

Libby studied each face in turn. Alan Jenkins from the garage, scrubbed and clean in his best suit, had removed every trace of oil. Samantha Watson leaned her head close to Chief Inspector Arnold, taking no notice of her husband, Ned, who stood on her other side. Angela, Marina, George, Beryl and the others from the local history society gazed at Libby, eyes wide. Bert, Elaine's husband, rested against the wall on the far side of the room, as far from his wife and daughter as possible.

Guy and the two Sutcliffes, father and son, stood a little apart from the townspeople, while Joe Ramshore took up a stance near the door, puzzled eyes fixed on Libby. She took a breath.

'Susie drowned, just like her daughter. It looked like an accident, or suicide. A woman still grieving for the loss of her daughter: who'd be surprised if she chose the same way to die? She was bruised. Again, you'd expect that, what with the way the sea lashed the shore on the night she died. It didn't prove she was murdered. But one thing made it certain.'

Feet shuffled. A forest of faces goggled at Libby. 'You all knew old Mrs Thomson. Lonely, missing her husband, she spent her days watching the world go by. She saw everything that happened on the beach, from her window. Some of you called her a nosy parker.'

More than one pair of eyes slid away. Libby said, 'You were right. Mrs Thomson watched what went on down at the beach, and she kept a diary. She saw the murderer dump the body under the lighthouse, that Monday evening, and she made a note of it, though she thought they were dumping a bag of litter. I found some of the notes in her house, but someone had been there before me. That person shoved the old lady down the stairs and took the notes, because they told us the name of the killer.'

In the sudden hubbub, Joe Ramshore pushed himself away from the door and cleared his throat. Libby shook her head. 'Luckily, the police didn't lock me up for removing the evidence. The notes were missing, but the murderer left behind the second sheet of paper from the pad, and we could make out the words.' Someone moved nearby. 'Unfortunately,' Libby went on, 'they were in Mrs Thomson's own brand of shorthand and she didn't write the full name of the murderer.'

'Well,' Samantha said. 'In that case, we're no further forward.' Her voice rang with disdain. 'Perhaps you should leave the investigation to the police, Libby. After all, they know the town. You've only lived here five minutes.'

'But she's been a good friend to us,' Mandy's voice shook with rage. 'Better than you, with your posh clothes and—'

Libby waved a hand. 'It's all right, Mandy. Samantha does have a point. I haven't lived here long, but as an outsider, perhaps I could see what was going on more clearly than the rest of you.'

She waited for the murmurs to die down. She couldn't care less if people thought she was interfering. Susie deserved justice. 'At first, we suspected Susie's husband. We thought he might have a financial motive, but we were wrong. They were divorced, legally, although against Susie's will. He wasn't entitled to her money.'

Faces that had brightened briefly, fell again. The townspeople wanted Mickey to be the murderer, so everyone else would be off the hook. Libby continued to talk.

'In any case, why would Mickey attack Susie in England? Wouldn't it have been far easier to have his wife killed in his own country?'

She had their full attention. 'I found Susie. I owed her something, and I wanted to know more about her. What she was like when she lived here, in Exham, where she died? Why was she killed here? Why now, when she'd come home?'

Libby's throat was dry. She took a sip of water, listening to the awkward shuffle of feet, the sharp intakes of breath. 'Everyone I spoke to filled in another part of the jigsaw. I discovered the men here seemed to like Susie, but the women didn't.' Someone giggled and was hushed.

'I heard how Susie left Exham in a hurry, and I began to wonder why. Max tracked down her daughter's birth certificate, and sadly, found another – for her death. I looked at Annie Rose's date of birth, and the date of Glastonbury that year, and realised Susie must have been pregnant before she left Exham. That led to another question. Did the father know about the child? What would he do, if he ever found out?'

She had everyone's full attention, now. 'At last, I understood. Susie's murder had nothing to do with money. It was about Annie Rose: about children, parents and jealousy. Susie loved Annie Rose – that's why she carried a child's plastic ring in her pocket until the day she died. I found Annie Rose's ring, with Susie, on the beach.'

'The murderer reckoned without Mrs Thomson. She knew everyone in town, and she recognised the murderer. In the twilight, as the sun went down, she saw someone she knew, carrying what looked like a sack of rubbish and leaving it under the lighthouse. That's what got her killed. She had no idea of the importance of what she'd seen, but the murderer caught sight of her, in the window of her house.

'Mrs Thomson left a clue, but it was tricky to decipher. When she made her rough notes, you see, she used an initial, as she always did, to remind her what she'd seen when she came to write up her diary.'

Libby raised her voice, to make sure everyone in the room heard. 'The killer's name begins with B.'

She waited as first one head, then another, turned, every horrified face pointing in the same direction. It was Alan Jenkins who blurted out the name. 'Bert Parsons.'

29

ANCESTORS

Mandy's mother screamed; the sound muffled by a clenched fist stuffed into her mouth. Bert raised red-rimmed eyes. 'It wasn't me, Elaine.'

Alan said, 'We all know you're not afraid of a spot of violence.'

Bert's head flicked from one side to the other, searching in vain for a friendly face. 'No-no. I didn't k-kill Susie,' he stammered. 'I never even went out with her. I was about the only one that didn't. I was already with you, Elaine. You know that. We got married just after we left school.'

Elaine ran at her husband, outstretched fingers curled like a cat's. 'That doesn't mean you weren't going with Susie at the same time.'

'Wait.' Max's voice rang out, and Elaine stopped in her tracks.

Libby said, 'Bert seemed a very likely suspect, but I saw a photo of Susie's daughter in Mrs Thomson's album. Annie Rose was very fair, with blonde hair and blue eyes.'

'That proves it.' Bert pointed at his own head. He was turning bald, the remaining hair thin, but still dark brown, almost black. His eyes were brown, like Mandy's. 'She can't be my daughter.'

Marina said, 'It doesn't prove anything. Susie had blonde hair, so of course Annie Rose did.'

'No.' Angela stepped forward. 'Not necessarily. Susie had blonde hair when she was small, but hair often darkens as you get older. Don't you remember at senior school? Susie's hair began to turn brown when she was about fifteen. She was devastated, and she started dyeing it. All that blonde hair came out of a bottle.'

Libby raised a hand to interrupt the arguments. 'Angela's right. Anyone can dye their hair any colour they choose, but Annie Rose's hair was unusually light in colour, sandy really. What combination of genes would give her such pale hair? And she had very blue eyes. Not green, or hazel, but bright blue. Her colouring doesn't rule Bert out, but maybe he wasn't the only man having an affair with Susie just before she left town.'

She looked straight at Samantha. 'Tell me, Samantha. What's Ned's real name?'

Samantha's head jerked up, face contorted. 'Wh-what do you mean? Ned, his name's Ned.'

'No, Samantha.' Angela said. 'Ned's family thought themselves a cut above the rest of us, descended from ancient Scots and the former owners of Mangotsfield Hall. They wouldn't give their son an ordinary name, worker's name, like Ned.'

Every eye was on Angela. 'I remember the day we started primary school, when the teacher took the register for the first time. She read out his name and we all laughed. Ned cried; he was so embarrassed.' She put an arm around Samantha's shoulder. 'Samantha, my dear, I'm afraid you already know this. Ned's real name is Benedict.'

Wild eyed, face purple, Ned stared from one face to another. With a roar, like an animal in pain, he dashed for the door. Guy stuck out a foot and Ned fell, heavily, on the plush carpet.

Samantha said. 'Your hair's that pale, sandy colour, or it used to be, before you lost most of it. It's your Scottish family.'

Libby said, 'Most people had forgotten you were called Benedict, but Mrs Thomson always used full names. In her mind, Susie was always Suzanne, and Max was Maxwell. To her, you remained Benedict, even when everyone else called you Ned.'

Joe Ramshore tightened his grip on one of Ned's arms. Max had grabbed the other, but after that first dash for freedom, Ned gave up the struggle. He was crying, his words muffled by sobs.

'I never knew Annie Rose was my baby. Susie should have told me.' He cried louder, 'I never knew I was a father.'

He took a long, shuddering breath. 'Susie came back to England, to see Mary Sutcliffe, James's wife. Mary was dying. Susie was her friend, and she wanted to see Mary one last time. I bumped into her in Bristol.' He wiped his nose on his sleeve. 'She still looked the same: still the Susie I'd loved. She never really cared much for me – anyway, not once she'd met that American and been swept off her feet. We met up, just for a drink, one night. Not around here – we went over to Wells. Susie didn't want people to see her in the Lighthouse Inn.' He glared at Samantha. 'You were out with your fancy man, that policeman, pretending to be at work. You must have thought I was stupid.'

Chief Inspector Arnold stepped closer to Samantha and slipped an arm round her shoulders.

Ned's lip curled. 'I drove Susie back to Bristol. She'd had a lot to drink, and it loosened her tongue. She told me everything. All about my little girl: how cute she was, that Mickey never really took much notice of her, and how she died all alone in that swimming pool. I think I went a bit crazy. I couldn't think straight.'

Libby strained to hear Ned's words through his tears. 'Susie had taken my little girl away and left her with a man who let her die. I was so angry; it was like they say in stories – a red mist in front of my eyes.'

He raised his head. 'I wanted to avenge the daughter they stole from me.' He stood tall, his head straight on the broad shoulders Mrs Thomson had recognised. 'I grabbed the Satnav and hit Susie with it. It smashed into the side of her head. I hadn't even stopped the car – it skidded all over the road before I got my foot on the brake. I could have been killed, as well.' He rubbed clenched fists into his eyes. 'All I could think of was my little girl, drowning. Susie deserved to pay for Annie Rose's death.'

He took a breath, shuddering. 'I drove to Exham, pulled out a bin liner from the boot of the car, put her in so no one would see her, and carried her out to the beach. It was already blowing a gale and she was heavier than I thought. I left her under the lighthouse; tucked her in between the supports. I didn't kill her. I gave her a chance – left it to fate to decide. She might have woken up in time, before the tide came in.' He looked at the ring of horrified faces and pleaded, 'I didn't kill her. You can't call me a murderer.'

A burst of anger overcame Libby. 'How dare you. You didn't just kill Susie – you pushed a helpless old woman down the stairs and tried to poison poor Bear.'

The look on Ned's face chilled Libby's bones. 'That stupid old woman, watching everything, telling tales. She deserved all she got.'

He sneered at Libby. 'I saw her looking out of the window. I hoped she hadn't realised what was going on. She was a decrepit old bag – I thought she couldn't know who I was, even if she knew it was Susie in the bag.

'But it nagged at me – did my head in. What if she did know – what if she went to the police.'

He shrugged, cold eyes glittering. 'There was only one thing to do – get rid of her. It was easy enough – one little shove and she somersaulted down the stairs.'

He chuckled, the sound sending a shudder through Libby. 'You were lucky, Mrs Forest. You and your fancy ways – my aunt told me you were at the old woman's place.'

'Your aunt?' Libby screwed up her eyes, trying to think. 'Oh, the woman who visited Mrs Thomson while I was there. She's your aunt?'

Max said, 'I told you, half the town is related to the other half.'

Ned hadn't stopped talking, saliva flying from his mouth as he spat the words out. 'I came to your house to finish you off, but that stupid dog made such a racket, I didn't get the chance.' He swore. 'What do you mean by coming here, lording it around town, making out you're better than the rest of us?'

'That's enough.' Joe pulled Ned away. 'We've heard more than enough to get you put away for years.'

'How could you do such things, Ned?' Samantha called, as Ned was led away. 'How could you kill two people?'

Ned glowered at his wife, hate in his eyes. 'They deserved it. I wish I'd made it three.'

Libby curled up on the sofa while Max stretched out in an armchair. Both nursed large glasses of wine. Bear and Fuzzy jostled for position on the floor, in front of the fire. Mandy had taken her mother back to Bristol on the train. 'I'll be back the moment she starts nagging,' she whispered to Libby. 'Her sister can look after her. See you tomorrow, probably.'

'The town will pay for Susie's headstone,' Max said. 'It's going to say, *Loving Mother of Annie Rose.* We won't take the money from her estate. Everyone wants to chip in.'

'I'm glad about that. I'm sure Annie Rose was all Susie really cared about in the end. If only she'd known how many people still cared about her.'

Max asked, 'How did you guess Susie was pregnant when she left Exham? You weren't here then.'

'I remembered dressing up in a Victorian costume at Mangotsfield Hall. It was the costume, you see. There were layers of clothes; petticoats and skirts and corsets. I think I said, 'I could put on pounds and no one would notice.' The point was, you could hide anything under there. It rang a bell, because my son had told me about one of my husband's ancestors, a maid, who "got into trouble". But I didn't put it all together at first. I didn't think about Susie hiding her bump to trap Mickey into marrying her and then believing he was Annie Rose's father.'

She took a large mouthful of wine. 'About you.' Max raised his eyebrows and he looked wary. 'You loved Susie.'

He nodded. 'You're right again,' he said. 'Bert, Mickey, Samantha, Ned. You've understood them all. You're right about me, too. I never quite got over Susie. I met my wife in Bath, but our marriage was a mistake. Joe grew up living with my wife. I don't think he ever forgave me, even though she was the one who left. Divorce is tough on a child.' He shrugged. 'I concentrated on my career, made some money on the stock exchange – quite a lot, as a matter of fact – enough to buy my house, and the Thomson's farm, and retire. But there was always something missing. I grew bored.'

He smiled. 'I looked around for something else to do – something that could give me the buzz banking lacked. I found some consultancy work. I'm something of a whizz with figures. I specialise in following financial trails, tracking how money moves from one hand to another, and how criminals hide it inside legitimate businesses. I love travel, and I have clients all over the world.'

Libby smiled. 'Including America. You were going over on business as well as seeing Mickey.'

He laughed. 'I took the opportunity to visit one of my clients, as well as our friend Mickey.'

Bear raised his head, lurched to his feet and collapsed with a sigh at Libby's feet. She leaned over to stroke him. 'Tell me about Alan Jenkins. I know he's one of your old mates, but you wouldn't have been able to get him out of trouble with the police if you didn't have contacts.'

'You're quite a sleuth, Libby. The ringing gang was part of a vehicle fraud, where the proceeds were laundered and sent to Latin America to finance the drug trade. Joe discovered it, and he was on the point of arresting poor Alan, who had no idea what he was getting into. An innocent, is Alan Jenkins – he's happiest with his cars. I did some research into the gang and persuaded Joe to drop the case against Alan, in return for information. It was a pretty flimsy case, anyway. Joe's bosses were far more interested in the men behind the fraud and didn't want to expose them too soon. They'll be arrested, soon enough.'

'That gave Joe another reason to be mad at you. No one likes their parents interfering at work.'

Max drained his glass. 'True. I'm not easy to know, Libby. You'll find that, if you let me stick around.' He stood up. 'Do you want me to go now, and let you get on with your new life? What's it going to be: writing books, or a chocolatier, or both?'

Libby's body ached with tiredness. Her brain had all but stopped working, but at least she knew she didn't want Max to disappear from her life.

'I don't know at the moment, but I'll think about it all tomorrow. For now, let's just finish the wine.'

ACKNOWLEDGMENTS

I've loved writing this, the first Exham on Sea mystery in the series. Many people helped me on the way with their support, from work colleagues who encouraged me to write, to my family who read and check every word.

A small army of readers have helped with all the Exham on Sea stories, reading early versions and offering wonderful advice, and many people I don't even know have boosted the book on its way with their reviews.

I'd like to thank my new publishers, Boldwood Books, for their confidence in me, and especially Caroline Ridding, for her rigorous editing and cheerful advice.

Finally, I'm most grateful to my long-suffering husband, for always being there, positive and encouraging, no matter how crotchety I become as I wrestle with my stories.

He also makes the very best cup of tea in the world.

MORE FROM FRANCES EVESHAM

We hope you enjoyed reading *Murder at the Lighthouse*. If you did, please leave a review.

If you'd like to gift a copy, this book is also available as an ebook, digital audio download and audiobook CD.

Sign up to become a Frances Evesham VIP and receive a free copy of the Exham-on-Sea Kitchen Cheat Sheet. You will also receive news, competitions and updates on future books:

https://bit.ly/FrancesEveshamSignUp

ABOUT THE AUTHOR

Frances Evesham is the author of the hugely successful Exham-on-Sea Murder Mysteries set in her home county of Somerset. In her spare time, she collects poison recipes and other ways of dispatching her unfortunate victims. She likes to cook with a glass of wine in one hand and a bunch of chillies in the other, her head full of murder—fictional only.

Visit Frances' website: https://francesevesham.com/

Follow Frances on social media:

twitter.com/francesevesham

facebook.com/frances.evesham.writer

bookbub.com/authors/frances-evesham

instagram.com/francesevesham

ABOUT BOLDWOOD BOOKS

Boldwood Books is a fiction publishing company seeking out the best stories from around the world.

Find out more at www.boldwoodbooks.com

Sign up to the Book and Tonic newsletter for news, offers and competitions from Boldwood Books!

http://www.bit.ly/bookandtonic

We'd love to hear from you, follow us on social media:

facebook.com/BookandTonic

twitter.com/BoldwoodBooks

instagram.com/BookandTonic

Ingram Content Group UK Ltd.
Milton Keynes UK
UKHW021312190423
420429UK00023B/962